Hijack Holiday

By Christina Starobin

Copyright© 2022 Christina Starobin
ISBN: 978-81-8253-895-5

First Edition: 2022
Rs. 200/-

Cyberwit.net
HIG 45 Kaushambi Kunj, Kalindipuram
Allahabad - 211011 (U.P.) India
http://www.cyberwit.net
Tel: +(91) 9415091004
E-mail: info@cyberwit.net

We hope that you will find yourself and the world in these pages but any resemblance to a person or event is accidental and not to be taken seriously..

Printed at VCORE CONNECT LLP.

THERE ARE NO RESTRICTIONS TO READING THIS BOOK

The following pages contain the narrative of DC flight 787 from JFK to Nassau in the Bahamas. The first section contains 40 personal histories told by some of the passengers and crew. The second section unfolds the events in which they were involved. As with all narratives, it is up to you to decide which narrators are reliable and which are merely self-serving, or, at worse, distorting the story for various purposes. Technical details have been altered so as not to provide a blueprint for terrorists.

Just a suggestion: it would be wise for you, as an impartial reader, to reserve judgment for as long as possible. Perhaps this might be said not only for the purposes of this narrative, but for your own lives as well.

Whenever we think we find what we're looking for, life changes so that this seeming solution no longer applies. However, it is also in the "scheme of things" to remind us exactly what is valuable when we are in situations of extreme stress and fear.

PASSENGERS

Ashad, Ali – 16 D
Beldez, Ethiopia – 30 D
Cologne, James – 18 C
Franklin, William – 24 E
Franklin, Topaz – 24 F
Hardcastle, Helmet – 28 F
James, Frank – 25 B
Krauss, Candy + service dog – 16 A & B
Krutz, Susan – 21 F
Lee, Wendy, Dr. – 11 F
Livingston, Karen – 21 A
Livingston, Olivia – 21 B
Lovehill, Helen – 20 B
Lovehill, Jesse – 19 A
Lovehill, Jonquil – 19 B
Lovehill, William – 20 A
Nash, Holly – 14 C
Nolan, Mike – 29 B
Sample, Cyd – 29 D
Sanchez, Sunny – 17 D
Solakis, Joseph – 16 D
Solakis, Mira – 16 E
Snark, Enid – 8 A
Spruce, Kathy – 29 A
Stein, Zedda – 7 F
Stewart, Evangeline – 25 A
Talenkov, Jake – 26 A
Walker, Buster – 27 D
Walker, Joline – 27 E

Wannamaker, Ethel - 28 C
Wardhope, Lucy – 28 B
Wardhope, Nancy – 28 D

LAW EFORCEMENT

Hackerstein, Henry – air marshal – 7 D
Dennison, Jerry – NYPD – 6 A
West, Hank – NYPD – 6 C
escorting Banks,Sam – 6 B

CREW

Bronze, Billy – co-pilot
Stark, Herb – pilot
Billings, Cynthia – flight attendant
Charles, Happy – flight attendant
Jameson, Caleb – custodial - JFK

14 C

Okay, so I'm still a little shaky. Well, maybe more than a little. If anyone else told me this I would have been terrified out of my skull. Then I would think it was something that they made up to freak me out. But no. It's true. I have been so careful and it worked. All that planning paid off.

You know the ancient Greeks and Romans had something they called "deus ex machina" which meant "God from a machine" which they used in their plays; it was a crane that would propel a god as if from the sky into the action of a play to provide the ending. It's come to mean an artificial ending to a seemingly impossible situation.

Well, being in an airplane is the reverse of this: instead of the god being lifted up by a machine, you are lifted up by the machine and then your little mundane mind has to deal with that fact. You are transported to a place where your problem can disappear because you have disappeared and you're not where people could be looking for you. You will arrive somewhere as if by magic and you will not be the same. Guaranteed. It's like a drug trip but instead of buying a pill you're buying a ticket. And suddenly nothing is the same. Does this make me feel like a goddess? Well, maybe a little bit.

This has got to be the best feeling. Sitting in the plane, waiting to take off, luggage all checked, passed through the airport maze. Being SCANNED in the big ARC D'TRIOMPHE . My jewelry: my watch into the x-ray tray, my silver bracelets and then, the piece du resistance, my hair barrette (which I don't know why they didn't see) starts the beeping. Beep, beep, beep. And I can see everyone looking at me and me feeling like there's nowhere I can run.

I mean they did ask me to take off my hat. So why didn't they look at the top of my head? I mean I'm not exactly TALL? So I took off the barrette and the beeping stops. Be still my heart.

And then the shoes! Taking them off and balancing on one foot without falling over, the pressure of everyone behind you waiting to take off their shoes. Getting all the gunk from the airport on your socks. Uggh! Not to mention having to finish all the water in the water bottles I have just purchased because you CAN'T BRING WATER INTO THE PLANE, it might be an explosive? Come on. Don't they think the terrorists are already smarter than that? Haven't they already gotten past us when it really mattered?

Never do they imagine that someone with something to hide will throw a red herring into the mix, get caught for some small article (like my barrette, for instance) so that they can escape serious suspicion.

But planning sure paid off. I have my regulation suitcase (checked), my smaller bag which is my carryon bag and then my tote bag, which counts as my handbag, but really it's just stuffed with all my essentials: passport, medications for my asthma in boxes with the doctors' Rx on them, which I won't be able to duplicate if they get lost in Mexico, my book for the plane, my diary, my extra jewelry which I cannot afford to lose if the bag gets misplaced. I know I'm chattering. I do that when I'm nervous.

Now the hard part is over. And I'm in the plane early so there's still plenty of room and I can take the aisle seat which is mine anyhow. I'm in the plane, my bags are in the plane, I have packed coordinating outfits which don't take up too much room. This is the part of travel I adore. All year long I watch the TV shopping channels advertise luggage and outfits that pack well and I never go anywhere. I buy outfits "just in case" but I don't go. NOW I AM GOING. And it took a break up with the love-hate monster of five years to get me out of New York City. I'm saying breakup but it was the end of a marriage which is much more serious. I don't know if they have a word for it. "Divorce" is too cliché; it's the end of a way of life.

Really, it was the hardest thing I have ever done. It took me a year to decide to leave Sport. I thought about it and thought about it. I didn't mention it to anyone. Finally his relatives, who I absolutely adore, said, "We like you but we'd like you better without Sport." I figure that they have to be trying to tell me something. You know, I kept thinking he would change. People believe that about marriage. "After we're married, it'll be different." But it isn't. If anything, it's worse, because now you know that marriage isn't going to change it.

I don't want to say "Once a junkie always a junkie". I mean I got over many problems and I do believe that you can get over an addiction if you want to. But Sport didn't want to. Of course, he did sell dope, in moderate amounts, so maybe that had more to do with it than I wanted to admit. I kept thinking it was my fault. If only I were a better person, a cuter person, a more patient person, a sexier person, a more intelligent person, he would change. But that had nothing to do with it

I mean I was reading Proust, Proust for goodness sake. And when we would go to his connections' houses I would talk to everyone who was waiting for their drugs about Proust, Remembrance of Things Past, all seven volumes. I would tell them interesting anecdotes and I do believe they were interested. And when we left Sport would say, "Do you really think anyone was interested in what you have to say? Do you?" Or if I told a joke he'd say, "Do you really think that joke was funny?" It got so I was afraid to open my mouth. I would start to say something and then I would doubt myself and I started to stutter. I never stuttered in my life before, but this was the effect Sport's criticism had on me. I knew it because I could feel the hesitation and uncertainty in my mind as I started to speak. That was when I knew I had to leave him.

But I learned something from him. I guess there's a little more larceny in my soul than he imagined. I'm going to Mexico, how perfectly lucky and I deserve it, I deserve it, I DESERVE IT! First a stop off in the Bahamas to throw them off the track. And I've fixed it so that THIS TRIP WILL PRACTICALLLY PAY FOR ITSELF. He will not discover that I took his money. He'll think it was the other connection. He didn't even realize I knew where he kept his precious dough. So he won't come looking for me. The other connection will think Sport stole their money and go looking for him. They were having issues before this so their first thought will be to accuse each other. They will be so busy figuring out who is double crossing whom first that it will never occur to them to think of a GIRL. How clever am I? I mean, I guess they might send someone to look for me, if they figure out it was me, that is. But what are the chances of that?

Does this mean I'm as rotten as he is? Or does it just mean survival of the cutest? Uggh. Maybe the things I hated about him have become part of me; that's how I could even think to pull this off.

Enough analysis. I packed that wonderful yellow jump suit with the bare shoulders and matching cotton heavy lace around the top. Yum! And with my turquoise earrings and the straw tote that packs up flat. My sandals. And I've taken lots of suntan lotion because that is sooooo expensive when you get to a resort. I will lie on the beach in a lounge chair and sunglasses, I'll get a big hat when I get there, my flip flops, my new mystery novel, and I will soak in the calming rays. And then the bus tours of Chichen Itza. Wow! Magnificent silver jewelry. And I've saved up extra ready cash to buy myself some nice gifts, and, of course, earrings for all the girls, a pin for my mom. Oh, I so need this to relax and finally draw a deep breath on my life.

I still feel like I'm looking over my shoulder. Well, that should pass, presently.

21 A & B

"KAREN! KAREN! Where are you? KAREN! Here she comes. Finally. What do you think? I like to be left alone? Like I don't matter?"

"Livy, I told you I would be gone ten minutes. I had to use the rest room."

"Some ten minutes. Now where are we going?"

"We're going to Freeport, to see Cecille and Harvey." Pause. "We're going to live with them."

"Oh, why? I don't remember them inviting us. What about my house?"

"Remember we had to sell your house. The taxes were too high. You were the first one to point that out and you were right."

"Oh. Well, where are we going now?"

"We're on a plane. We should be there in three hours. They will meet us at the airport and take us to our new home. They have rooms all ready for us."

"I don't know."

"And the weather will be so much better than Long Island. Remember the hurricanes we've been having? We just can't go through with that again. And you can see the grandchildren any time."

"I suppose."

"Do you want to use the restroom?"

"Why do you keep asking me that? If I want to use the restroom I'll let you know. I didn't reach 92 years of age because I forgot how to use the restroom."

"Just trying to be helpful. Do you want to eat something?"

"Don't they serve meals on planes?"

"Not anymore. Not if you're not in first class. And we're not in first class. But we bought those nice sandwiches at the terminal and they will give us a beverage."

"Seems they should do a whole lot more for the prices they charge."

"Did it upset you going through all the searches before we got on the plane? That must have been upsetting."

"I liked it! I love taking off my shoes and showing strange men my feet! So much attention! I don't know what they thought they would find."

"Glad you're enjoying yourself. Do you want a pillow? We brought those inflatable pillows, travel pillows."

"Yes, thank you. Put it right behind the small of my back."

"Just a minute, I have to blow it up first."

"Did you bring one for yourself? I don't want to hog the pillows."

"Yes, Livy, I brought the green one for me and the yellow one for you. There, how's that?"

"Better. Don't they ever get this plane off the ground? How do they expect to get there if they don't get off the ground?"

"I think there are some planes ahead of us."

"When do we get the beverages?"

"I don't know. We have to take off first. I think we also get peanuts or a snack."

"Great. What if you're allergic? Do they ever think about that?"

"I think they have some gluten free snacks."

"I think for these prices they should keep the gluten in. Did you put all the luggage on the plane?"

"We checked two bags and we have two in the overhead. And we have two totes here."

"What about that extra bag you brought?"

"I didn't bring an extra bag, Livy."

"Yes, you did, Karen. I remember because it didn't look like any of our luggage. Did you leave it in the airport?"

"I didn't bring an extra bag."

"Don't pretend like I don't know what's going on. There were seven bags, I counted them. You say you checked two, two overhead and two totes in the cabin. One bag is missing."

"Don't exert yourself, Livy. We've got all our luggage. There's nothing to worry about."

"You'd think that with all this stuff going across country you would try to keep track."

"You're just thinking of the things we had shipped."

"Karen, I know what I'm thinking. Don't try to make it like I'm stupid. I'm not stupid. I didn't get to be 92 by being stupid. And I know that guy you're seeing that you pretend is just the UPS man."

"He is the UPS man."

"Then why does he come in the middle of the night?"

"He doesn't come in the middle of the night, Livy!"

"What day is it? What time is it?"

"It's two o'clock."

"In the morning?"

"No, the afternoon."

"But it looks so dark."

"That's because people put down the shades on the window to cut the glare of the sun."

"Oh, and what day is it?"

"It's Friday. We'll be in Nassau in three hours."

"I hope we don't get in trouble for leaving the bag in the airport. Why aren't we getting started? We've been here much too long."

"Here, Livy, just relax. Everything will be fine."

"Whenever anyone says that, it's a sure sign of disaster. That's what they said to my sister before they took out her left lung."

7 D

I don't think anyone spotted me in the terminal. Just another middle aged businessman with a briefcase and a raincoat. I got a coffee, I used the restroom. No one was following me or seemed alert to my movements. Always such a war of nerves.

I don't know why I took this job, I really don't. The money, the money, it's always the money. I guess it's as good an excuse as any. It's certainly something I can tell my wife, sweet Henriette, and that she'll blame me for if it goes wrong.

"Henry," she'll say, "money is not worth your life. Any dollar bill looks like any other, but an hour lost is lost forever and you'll never find another like it. " Easy for her to say, she's not paying the major bills.

That fear of not being able to pay—for medication, for housing, the assisted living—the fear that money will run out and you will have nowhere to turn just destroys you. Your house will be taken, you won't be able to live anymore, never mind not getting medical treatment. And once you experience it the slightest whiff of financial panic brings it back—blind terror. You freeze. You'll do anything, like a trapped animal, to be able to get free. Anyone who offers advice, who seems to provide the glimmer of an answer, is suddenly your salvation.

I got in touch with the people at Office for the Aging for Henriette's care. As soon as they found out I had a salary, they wanted to take all my assets. "You can just turn it all over and we'll pay the bills," they said. "I have two pieces of advice for you," they said. "Keep your mouth shut and keep smiling." I'd like to give them a piece of advice but it's not something that they could repeat.

Still, I am not trying to complain about the medical establishment; that happens naturally.

Why is everyone always feeling put upon? Like they're entitled to something more. "It's coming to me: the raise/promotion/new car/tax break is coming to me." I don't think we were brought up that way. A job, as my father used to say, was something you didn't like. We did not grow up seeing snippy teenagers conning their parents out of money or new cars or trips to a tropical island.

That tropical island bit, I know Henriette would have loved to come along. "It's too dangerous," I told her. "Nothing is worth you risking your life."

"But you're risking it," she said. I didn't know what to answer. I just kept packing my carry-on.

"And we could have a vacation."

"But I don't get to have any vacation. I go one way, have a day lay over and turn around and go back."

"Seems to me you should have it like the stewardesses, have some fun."

"Oh, would you like me to have a fast lifestyle? A girl in every airport? Love 'em and leave 'em Henry?"

She collapsed in laughter. I guess my face isn't exactly the Clark Gable type. More like Clark Griswold from National Lampoon.

Still she doesn't comprehend the risk involved; just the boring element of the job leaves you open to risk. You get to think everything is routine, ho hum, just going along and you miss the signs that spell disaster. That's why they pay me the big bucks. I'm always alert. That's also why I have the beginnings of an ulcer and can't get to sleep on these long flights. They say most accidents occur within five miles of your home. The minute you start to relax and think things are going along fine, that's when you're in big trouble.

Where is my magazine? Oh, I forgot to pack it. I think I took a paperback. Yes, short stories by Poe. I just love that guy. No matter how many times I read him he still knocks me out. You never get Poe relaxing and thinking things are going to be alright. No siree. Behind every tree lurks a demon, inside every house is a monster plague waiting to wipe out the human race. What is "The Masque of the Red Death" but a portrait of ebola? For Poe it was based on TB, what his mother died of, but today it could just as easily be ebola.

Reminds me, remember to wash hands thoroughly after the rest room and not to touch anything unnecessary. Don't want to bring home any viruses.

I really don't think they checked my carry-on thoroughly this time. If that is how conscientious they are with the other passengers I could have a real problem on my hands. Let me make a mental note of that.

Thank goodness they're not serving meals anymore. Fewer diseases to worry about. I don't know what cleanliness lessons they give these flight attendants; I certainly wouldn't want them taking charge of my kids or my home.

Now I am beginning to get nervous. We are definitely not moving. And the seatbelt sign is on. A mistake on the part of the pilot? Or the computer? Will it matter if we go down in flames? I know I have the extra insurance and Henriette and they boys will be taken care of. I have learned to accept that as part of the job.

"You know paranoids make the best office workers," she said to me. "They're always worrying about things being found out so they go over and over their work." And then she gave me one of those looks. She is damn grateful for my paranoia when it comes to washing the dishes and tidying up, let me tell you.

I can't seem to concentrate. Maybe I shouldn't have had that coffee in the terminal. Still I can't afford to fall asleep. It's such a delicate balance between wakefulness and super vigilance. I have to strike the right balance or I'll go overboard one way or the other: either start to doze or start chewing the inside of my mouth with tension.

I don't think anyone made me in the terminal, just another raincoat with a briefcase. But not for long.

29 A & B

"Is my arm in your way? I can never figure out which armrest belongs to which seat."

"You're fine. What are you reading? It looks interesting."

"Just a mystery. I like to keep track of the plots. On the TV too."

"I love mysteries. Are you a writer?"

"Yes. And I do write mysteries."

"Do tell."

"Just about the most mysterious thing that happened to me recently was pretty scary. You probably wouldn't be interested."

"Well, this plane doesn't seem to be going anywhere. Try me."

"Okay. I almost killed a little boy."

"What? Are you serious? Is this a plot for a story?"

"No, I mean in my car. I almost ran over a little boy with my car."

"Whew! You really had me going there. What happened?"

"Well, I was on this country road that I am not that familiar with doing about 55 mph and out of nowhere jumps this little boy of about seven. Luckily I slammed on the brakes."

"Was he injured?"

"I was more shook up than he was. I pulled over and asked him what he was doing, where he lived. I mean we were in the middle of nowhere."

"And?"

"And I drove him to his house, which was only about half a mile away, but no one was home. Turns out his grandfather was in the next house so I went in. They had been looking for the boy for about half an hour. His folks started out to see a movie at the mall thinking he was in the back seat. And when they got there little Sammy was missing. Well, they were frantic. Everyone was happy that I bought him back."

"So it was a mystery with a happy ending."

"But that feeling, that feeling when you think you hit someone or almost hit someone—that is the most horrifying thing. It makes you shiver down to the bottoms of your feet. You can't imagine."

"Oh, yes I can. I had that feeling recently, too. I am a designer of sportswear."

"Really? Would I possibly be wearing anything you designed?"

"Well, maybe the vest might qualify."

"Really? Now you've got me interested. Go on."

"Well, I designed a line of sports tops and coordinating bottoms and brought them to a prominent manufacturer. They looked the designs over, but said they couldn't find anything they could use. I was disappointed; I thought I had a shot.

"Then I was with a friend and we went to the trade show in the Javits Center. There was a display for the company I had tried to sell to. We went in and there were my designs. All 18 of them. They didn't even change the colors."

"Was there nothing you could do?"

"Well, I tried to take legal action. And finally they did make a settlement,"

"How much, might I ask? $1,500?"

"$1,000."

"How awful!"

"Yes, and that sinking feeling in your stomach, like someone just sucker punched you, that feeling, yes, I know it well."

29 D & E

My dad always wanted to be in a hijacked plane. He had worked as a reporter after World War II in Europe. When he met my mom he was a reporter in Central and South America.

After he got his Masters and PhD, which he did while working during the daytime when I was in high school, he got a series of better paying jobs as an economist. One job was for a television manufacturer and when the president of that corporation became ill they asked my dad to take his place for a while.

In that capacity he went back and forth between the US and Japan for conferences on the manufacture of the components, often meetings about how far apart the knobs on the consoles should be and other more technical matters. In a period of three years he made 46 trips to Japan and each trip he made it a point to see some special place in the country he had never seen before. For a man who disliked visiting the churches in Europe he made up for it with the number of shrines he visited in Japan.

He also had a deep understanding of the culture of the country and was the person called upon when the Japanese employees in the US were not comfortable here. I recall the story of one man who locked himself in his hotel room and when my dad was summoned it turned out this man wanted someone to go and eat noodles with; just a simple familiar act made him feel at home but only my dad was able to reach him. Together they ate noodles.

When my father went to and from Japan he visited the homes of the Japanese plant owners. My mother, a professional puppeteer, made finger puppets for the children of the Japanese managers. In Japan handmade gifts are more valuable than store bought ones. They gave my family a TV as a thank you gift. "We know you have a TV in every room; maybe you can put this one in the bathroom," they said to him. Needless to say, it was the best TV we ever had.

All the trips my dad made involved him packing his own bags, which he had down to a science, being driven to the airport (JFK) and, upon returning, calling my mom from the airport. "The eagle has landed," he would say. When he got to call me he would begin with the statistics: "We were held on the runway for one and one half hours going there. On the way back we had to wait two hours in the airport." The total time he spent waiting on all his business trips together could have made a nice two week family vacation.

All the time there were numerous hijackings of planes, especially the international flights, yet never once did they happen upon the plane on which my father was a passenger. I think it's the law of the universe that whatever you yearn for will elude you and whatever you shun will turn up and tap you on the shoulder.

I longed to be able to follow in his winged footsteps, so to speak. It was also his karma to be out of the country when members of our family died. And perhaps it was ironic that when he died my boyfriend and I were vacationing hundreds of miles away only to be brought back by an unexpected phone call.

Now, since I've taken up enough of your time, I think it only fair that you tell me about one of your family members. Go on, there's lots of time. We seem to be delayed unexpectedly and I'm just sitting here waiting. Don't be shy. We'll probably never meet again so feel free to tell me a really good story. I'm all ears.

18 C

What the hell. I mean you can't even relax and get drunk on a plane anymore, you have to worry about whether they're going to find bomb making chemicals in the luggage. Maybe that's what's delaying us. Some kind of tip about something in the luggage.

And no good meals, overcharging for every fucking thing. What's the use of being free white and 21 if you can't have a good time when you fly, for god's sake?

I work my butt off to get this goddamn degree at the computer fucking institute, not the TV commercial but one better. And I get trained by the guy who put a monitor inside the monkey cage at the zoo to keep track of the fucking animals. I might as well have turned myself into a monkey for all the good it does me.

Now the guys who did the nature show on the meerkats in Africa, there was some sweet deal. Set up a camera and take pictures of little furry monsters, each with their own tracking device and then rake in the dough. All they had to do was figure where to put the camera and what names to give them. Then they got the guy from LORD OF THE RINGS to narrate, what was his fucking name? Hell, I would have put a tracking collar on myself and hid in the little burrows if it got me that publicity.

It's all about being there first. And the way this plane is going no one is getting anywhere first.

There's a cute chick, the one with the long dark hair. All that silver Native American jewelry. She looks like she might be fun. She looks a little spacey but that's so much the better. They don't keep track. They're not clicking inside the head with the adding machine, "How much he spent on me, how much he makes, how much will the wedding cost, how much does he spend on his clothes," and like that. It's enough for them to count the number of drinks they're drinking, if they can do that.

I mean, I'm not a chauvinist pig, I'm not any kind of pig. I like a girl to look nice and not be all the time, "Do I look fat? Do my boobs look OK? Am I as pretty as your last girl friend?" and all that shit. And I don't want her crawling up inside my head with all that relationship crap.

Hey, she's looking my way. I'll give her my sun glasses down the nose, then a slow smile. That always gets them. She's smiling. I'll just get up and see if she wants a drink.

"I'm sorry, sir, but the seat belt sign is on. You'll have to stay in your seat until take off."

Yeah, the stewardess. "Can you ask that young lady there if she wants a drink? Better still, just give her what she wants and charge it to me. And here's a little something for your trouble."

"Oh, sir, that's not necessary."

"Just keep it, I know what a pain these assholes on the plane can be," as I stuff the $20 in her pocket. Yeah, the smiling stewardess. "And give me a Jack on the rocks."

I nod at the chick with the raven hair, my little pretty Betty Blackbird. And I lift my glass to her. She pretends like she's embarrassed, but she's tickled down to her cuticles. Let's see some action here. Lucky I didn't stand up after all.

17 D

I'M FREE! I MADE IT! I'M FREE! I ESCAPED THOSE BLOOD SUCKING BASTARDS!

Getting on this plane was a freaking miracle. My god I owe sooooo much money. I am in debt to the connection such big bucks, not to mention the other thing. DON'T EVEN THINK ABOUT IT. That's done. No one will find me, no one will ever know where I have gone.

So CLEVER. Sooooooo clever. They would think "South America", they would think, "Mexico," but no. I am SUNNY SANCHEZ and I am smarter than all of them, those lousy coked up bastards that call themselves dealers.

I got just enough for me and then I'm going to kick. I did it before and I can do it again. No little Miss Smarty Pants to go along and fuck it up for me. Last time I was clean and it was her, the Princess, "Oh, Sunny, I just need a little more. I can't do it all the way this way. Just one more hit. I'll quit tomorrow." And I get all protective and get her a little more and the next thing I know I'm back with the needle in my arm and up to my nose in debt. And she just sits there, "I told you so. I knew you couldn't do it." Yeah, she knew. What a crock.

Well, I fixed her this time. I left her cold without a note, without any way for anyone to find out where I am going. That's all I need. She would crack under pressure, I know that. She's visiting her mother on Long Island and I hope she stays there for a good long while. 'Cause it's hasta la vista, baby, and she can cover her own lily white ass for a change.

How much money I spent on that one. I don't even want to think about it. Presents and birthday presents and anniversary presents and presents for her family and her no goodnick friends. Caramba! What a gigantic waste of time and money.

Yes, she was a good screw, but there will be others and right now the bottom line is the one my my ass is on. If they find out what I did. Well, they didn't. Otherwise I wouldn't even be on this plane.

They would have stopped me in the airport. Shit, they would have gotten me outside my apartment before I got into the cab. No, I'm safe. I made it. I can relax and have one of these high priced airplane drinks. Hallelujah! I'm on my way!

Sunglasses, a hat, and not just the hat I always wore. And I started to grow a little fuzz on the face. Great idea. A suit jacket, very conservative, nothing like I would ever wear before. No leathers. No cowboy boots. Cool it for a while. No point taking risks. I'm going in for something new.

Not that I'm afraid of risks. I remember when I was wanted by the police in Philly and I was staying with that Angela. I was just about to split town and I wake up that morning and look out the window and what do I see: an entire fucking parking lot full of MG's and Corvettes. "My friends" stole about 40 cars overnight and parked them outside so the police would HAVE to find me. I almost shit my pants, but I was cool. I made it out of there so fast you think someone greased my ass but good. And I threw the gun over the railing on the bridge on my way out. Those were some crazy times.

But somehow it doesn't seem like that anymore. No more fun and games, just heartache and stomach trouble. If I eat any more of those Tums I think I'll turn into a dispensing machine.

Where is that stewardess? She's not up front, let me just turn around. Shit. There's that girl that was going with Sport. Molly, Holly, Solly, I don't remember her name but that's her. Her hair is not the same color. What if they sent her to spy on me? Don't be paranoid.

It's just a coincidence. But what if it's not? What if she was put on this plane, and they knew my plan all along?

Cool it, Sunny. Just cool it. Don't even think about it. She probably didn't see you and maybe she won't recognize you. Shit, I've got to get off this plane. But that would be a sure way for them to find me. Maybe I could just slip off the plane. No, that's no good. We're already going down the runway. Goddamn. How to get out of this one?

Herb "Be Right" Stark, pilot

Yes, it certainly is a clear day for takeoff and I do hope they clear us soon. I'm dying to just sit back and let this auto-pilot coast for a while.

Hell, I've had a tough night, but I've had those before. It's all this new airport security that's getting to me.

When I had that flight to Ireland, that's one I'll remember for a long time. We had bomb threats but, of course, they didn't want to let on and upset the passengers. So they said there was an equipment problem and held take off for two hours.

I was still smoking then. You couldn't just get off the plane and grab a smoke. You had to go through all these check points, emptying out your pockets. Of course, it was different for the flight crew. Pity the poor bastards inside the terminal who wanted a smoke; they'd have to go out and then go through security again coming back in. And since we didn't know when we'd be taking off, no one wanted to risk going out for a smoke to come back and find out that the plane had boarded.

Well, finally we checked the plane through and determined that it was a false alarm. It was a nine AM flight to London and then a plane change, but because of the delay we had to make a stopover in London and put up everyone in a hotel overnight.

Everyone gets in those little buses to the hotel; it's really simple but because we got in so late everyone was tired. Then you can order breakfast, which is what I did—a big English breakfast with bacon, sausages, oatmeal, tea, muffins, the works. Only you don't get to eat it all because you've got to get on board earlier than the sun and start all over again.

I could have told them it was a false alarm. I always know. That's why they call me "Be Right" Stark. They're always secretly hoping that I'll be right.

I remember when I got the nickname. Again it was involved with the terrorists bombing. We were in the Southwest. It was early morning, after 9/11, of course, and the news came over the wires that there had been bombs in the London subway, "the underground". Everyone was worried it was the same people who had done the Twin Towers.

"No, it's a different group," I said with a confidence I hoped would be borne out.

"Oh, Herbie, I hope you'll be right," said my favorite stewardess.

"I hope so, too," I said. And I was.

And that wasn't the only time I was right. One flight after that we hit some pretty bad turbulence. There was the danger of part of the landing gear coming off. I said, "Don't tell the passengers; we'll be able to land fine even if it comes off."

"Oh, Be right, Herb," my second in command said.

And I was. It was pretty hairy, with the metal falling off in midair. I don't know if any of the passengers noticed it. We certainly did. But we landed fine anyhow. I was right again.

I hope I don't have to Be Right on this flight. But you never know.

14 C again

Well, it's about time we got into the air. I wonder how long I was going to have to keep waiting and waiting and waiting. Well, now that's cool.

I keep remembering Sport. He thought I was soooooo stupid. Just because I didn't go to an Ivy League school he thought I had no brains. I mean, it should have taught him something that I was reading Proust all the time. How many people living in LA are reading Proust? I mean, how many people in LA are reading at all? It's the original Tinsel Town and everyone is either at the movies, drinking before they go to the movies, drugging before and after they go to the movies or auditioning for a movie, or acting, or rehearsing, or going to a party with all the people from the movies.

I used to sit at that desk and everyone would see me reading. "Still reading THAT BOOK?" they would ask, without any idea of there being seven volumes in Proust. I could be on the fifth or the first, they wouldn't notice. At the bookstore they only had the first volume. "The kids have to read it for college, so they read the first and the last volumes," the bookstore guy said. And the bookstore didn't even have the last volume. I had to have him order it.

So I went to the library for the other volumes. When I got to the fifth volume they had to get it out of the attic. I mean no one ever read it. And the fifth was my favorite.

Anyhow, Sport was no judge of brains, no siree. And that's why I didn't have a hard time figuring out how to program computers. I just said to him, "Oh, it looks so complicated. How do you ever do it?" So he showed me, positive that I couldn't possibly be following. I mean, he was learning himself. And I picked up his books when he was out and

I went from there. I always had a good head for numbers. I was in advanced math in high school. And then I started really taking off so that I knew what was what before Sport even figured it out.

He just had no imagination. He always just thought so small. "I could program the bank's computers so that I could steal a little from each account and put it in a numbered account in a Swiss bank," he bragged. Like that hasn't been done in at least five movies including that cute comedy about office workers. But I can imagine. Just like Lennon said, "Imagine." That's what I did and that's what has gotten me where I am no and is going to get me even further. I'd love to see the look on his face when it all comes together.

That's what I enjoy. It's not so much the money, although that is nice, but being able to outsmart all those idiots who think what you see is what you get. A pretty girl cannot possibly be smarter than the big strong man. Oh, no. And their money is safe and their way of life is safe. They've got it all figured out. Well, let's just see what they say when this game goes up to the next level. Let's just see.

"Oh, thank you, stewardess. From that gentlemen where? Yes, I'll take a white wine, thank you." He looks cute. Smile at him, Holly. "Thank you!"

CYNTHIA BILLINGS and HAPPY CHARLES, flight attendants

"I swear, Hap, this flight is going to be my last."

"You say that every time, Cynthia, every time."

"This time I mean it. I gave notice."

"Really? Well, in that case do you want to go first with the cart this time?"

Cynthia nodded, straightened her tunic with both hands and tossed her head so that her medium sized dangle earrings settled themselves properly, not hanging backwards or touching the artistic wisp of dirty blonde hair.

"You go, girl," Happy said, putting a couple of extra ginger ales into the bottom shelf. As Cynthia moved down the aisle he took a moment to straighten up the back galley, stuffing stray plastic bags into the garbage slot. It was so much easier now that they didn't have to serve meals to anyone except the first class passengers. He followed Cynthia.

He admired her. Sure she was a little older and maybe the idea of retiring wasn't totally out of the question, but she didn't let anything faze her. He remembered that nutso passenger who kept leaning on the stewardess button like it was a TV control. "A human being is not a remote control device," was one of Cynthia's favorite expressions. Amen to that.

"Nuts or chips?" Happy asked the first set of passengers as Cynthia was pouring out their drinks.

"Do you have anything gluten free?" asked a cute brunette of maybe 35 by the window.

"As a matter of fact," Hap paused for effect, "these are absolutely free of anything. AND," another pause, "they actually taste good." He gave her a bag of the blue corn chips.

"Nuts for me," said the dour man next to her. Hap obliged.

They worked their way down the aisle, watching passengers who had to use the restrooms orient themselves to use the other side of the plane. The only trouble with not serving meals is that it made the flight that much longer, nothing to distract the passengers, Hap thought. He sighed.

When they got to the first class it was another story.

"Chicken or beef?" Cynthia asked, noting answers on her printed form.

"You're lucky to get anything at all," the man in blue said to the man in orange. The man in orange grunted.

"One grunt for chicken, two for beef!" the policeman on the other side of the convict joked. He laughed. Apparently he was enjoying this.

"You know, Hank, maybe you shouldn't have had that drink," the first policeman said to him.

"What drink? As far as the office goes I didn't have no drink," Hank brandished his plastic glass with ice and a sip of something.

"Yeah," said the first policeman.

"And just keep those no drinks coming," Hank raised his glass. The first policeman reached over the convict and pushed Hank's hand down.

"Quit, or he's not the only one who's going to be restrained." He looked at Hank firmly.

Hank hesitated a moment and then started laughing uproariously. "That's a good one, Jerry! You should have one yourself."

"No thanks, Hank, I don't like to drink."

"Why is that, Jerry?" Hank surveyed the passive face of his companion. He looked like a statue, Hank thought.

"Drink makes me silly," Jerry said evenly.

"Well, so loosen up a little. Get a little silly."

"I'm silly enough as is," Jerry said and settled back in his chair.

All through this the convict had not opened his eyes.

"And you remember that!" Hank laughed, as he poked the convict with his elbow. The convict opened his eyes and stared at Hank with mild amusement. He clamped his jaw shut and winced a broad smirk.

"I'd like some nuts," he said.

"You already got enough nuts!" Hank laughed.

"Open the package for him, Hank," said Jerry and he watched carefully, checking the hands in cuffs as Hank fumbled with the small package.

"We'll be back with your meals in a few moments," Cynthia said, keeping her eyes on the next row as she wheeled the drink cart slowly down the aisle.

"I can't believe everyone is so fussy," Happy remarked. "Or maybe it's just being on this water regiment that makes me super aware."

"Water regiment?" Cynthia asked.

"My doctor has me drinking ten glasses of water a day. "

"That's supposed to be good for you."

"Boring is what it is. Sometimes adding ice helps," Hap added.

"You know," she said to him as they turned the cart around to head down the other aisle, "what worries me?"

"No," said Happy moved out of the way of the outstretched legs in the aisles.

"You know how the policeman is going to retire and then he gets one last call the day before?" She looked over her shoulder to make sure Hap was listening. "And he goes on that call and gets shot?"

Happy nodded.

"Well, I'm thinking like that. For me this is that last flight. This is where the trouble happens. And I'm thinking maybe I should have made that decision before and stopped one flight back."

27 D & E

That's right, just act cool. No panic, everything nice and easy.

YOU'VE GOT THE MONEY! IT'S YOURS! ALL THE MONEY! Never thought I would actually get away with it. Just shows to go you.

"Yes, scotch rocks, please," Don't have too many. You don't want to get sloppy. And don't talk to anyone. That's a common mistake—bragging. How many robberies were ruined because someone shot their mouth off? Or started spending? No danger there. I made sure that I didn't get sequential bills, only robbed the deposit boxes.

And what a treasure is mine. Not only bills and certificates, but jewels. Of course, they will be harder to get rid of. And not easy to bring on the plane; that's why I overnighted them to myself at the hotel in Nassau and they should be there when I get there. Hallelujah!

Of course, I took a little token just for me, this totally undistinguishable diamond ring. Looks so big it looks fake. Just a plain setting. A nice little bauble for my pinky. But it's in my pocket for now; don't want to attract any attention.

I KNEW WHEN I STARTED WORKING AT THE BANK IT WOULD PAY OFF. BIG TIME. They needed an employee to fill their quota, but that didn't bother me. I worked my way up, month after month, year after year. And now I don't ever have to go back. Ever.

I told them I was going on my honeymoon. And so I am. Little Joline here is just as pleased as punch to be Mrs. Walker.

"Aren't you happy to be Mrs. Walker, sugar?"

"You know it, honey."

"Just show your daddy how much you appreciate all he's going to do for you. That's it, big kiss."

"You know it, honey."

Man, I never knew that robbery would spike my sex drive like this. She hasn't looked this good to me since the night I met her.

"Remember when we met, Joline?"

"I sure do. You were the best thing that ever walked into that diner."

"And what did I say to you? Do you remember?"

"You know I do. You said, 'I don't need a menu 'cause I know what I want and what I want is you.'" Giggles.

"And what did you say?"

"I said, 'You'd better have a big fat wallet because I am priceless.'" More giggles.

"And who has the fat wallet now, Mrs. Walker?"

"You do, my man."

"Yes I do! And that's what we both said, 'I do'!"

Giggles. "Oh, honey, I am so excited! I can't wait to get to the hotel!"

"You want to go into the restroom and get a little taste?"

Giggles. "You are so wicked! I've never seen you so excited like this!"

"Don't fight it, sugar, don't fight it."

"OK, Buster. I'll go in first and you follow."

"Just don't scream too loud; we don't want to attract attention."

"Oh, Buster, you are something else!"

"You ain't seen nothing yet, baby. You ain't seen nothing yet."

17 D again

Well, she turned and looked at me and she didn't even blink an eye.

Either she's a cool customer or she doesn't remember me. That wouldn't be surprising. She was stoned out of her mind half the time, if I remember right. She's cute and I know Sport would have killed anyone who came near her.

Too dangerous. Way too dangerous. If she doesn't know what I did to Sport and finds out she could get me iced for sure. If she does know, well, how do they say, my goose is cooked? Don't even think about it.

If only I could just stop my heart from racing so I could think clearly. I guess the coke I did before the flight sure didn't help. Did I ever do her? I know I did one of the chicks at Sport's but I think that was a red head. But maybe she changed her hair color. How I ever managed that—well, Sport was out of town. I went over there. It was a party, a few guys, a few chicks. I brought some coke. Soon everyone was high and I poured drinks for her and me.

Funny, she seemed taller, but she's sitting down, can't be sure.

Hey, Sunny, if you didn't use women like Kleenex or potato chips, or sports cars—hey, you wouldn't have problems. That was one thing about the Princess; she kept me on a short leash, except for a couple of occasions.

I curse the days I played around. I must really put on the brakes and not do that anymore or it will be my undoing. If I could only find a girl who was worth it. Yeah, that and give up drugs.

Well, this can be a new start for me. I might just be forced into kicking the habit due to lack of product with or without my best intentions.

Life can sure kick you in the balls when you least expect it.

29 A & B

"Thanks, I'll take the scotch. Anything for you?" Mike turned to Kathy.

"I'll have a diet Coke, thanks."

"A diet Coke for the lady, on the rocks. You sure you don't want something stronger? I mean I just met you but surely an airplane journey calls for celebration."

"Alright, I'll have a non-diet Coke."

The stewardess poured two drinks and reached over the open tray tables, maneuvering skillfully in the abbreviated space.

"Did you see that guy in the orange jumpsuit?" Kathy asked.

"You mean the one with the shackles on his feet and the handcuffs and the two policemen, one on either side? No, I hadn't noticed him." Both laughed.

"That's a little bit weird to me," said Kathy.

"Why?" Mike asked.

"Well, I guess I don't normally see a criminal in handcuffs and shackles on my plane flights. And with the two policemen."

"I guess you couldn't expect him to get on the plane and travel to his destination by himself," Mike said. Both laughed. "You think that's scary?"

"Well, a little bit. What if he breaks loose and does something like kidnap the plane?"

"I think it's called hijack and that's why the policemen are with him, I'd guess. You're thinking of a movie. But if you want to hear something scary let me tell you a couple of my scary bear stories."

"Are you a writer?"

"Nope."

"A hunter?"

"Nope, I just live in the country and that's where the bears are. Stewardess, (excuse me, Kathy, I just want to get her before she vanishes) can I get another of these?" He held out his folding money and the stewardess squeezed back a couple of rows.

"Better make it two," said Mike. "Anyhow my family had this place in the country ever since I was young and we used to come up on the weekends. The first time we went up, my mom had been getting the place ready so she was there before us. When she picked us up in the car she said, 'Now I don't want you to get upset but there have been some break-ins from wild animals this past week. Your two rooms (she meant my brother and me) both were broken into, and there might be some trace of the animal inside, but we patched up the windows for the time being. So don't worry.'

" 'Do you think it's bears?" my brother asked.

"'Don't know,'" she said, 'but don't worry. The windows are fixed.'

"We went to our rooms, opening the door carefully and looking around. I came out with this basket shaped like a baseball with candy in it. 'What's this?' I asked.

"'Must have been left by that notorious wild animal, the Easter Bunny!' she said with a big laugh."

Kathy smiled.

"But that was just the beginning. My mom loved songbirds and she put up this bird feeder. One night she's washing dishes late after dinner, about 11 o'clock, and she hears these chimes, wind chimes we also hung up. She suddenly realizes there is no wind. She looks straight out the window and there staring at her is this huge black bear, right on eye level. And the window, because the house is built on cinder blocks so there is drainage underneath, is at least six feet off the ground. She panicked."

"What did she do?" Kathy asked.

"For the moment, nothing. But the next day my dad went and took down the bird feeder which had been knocked down by the bear. The bear had pulled open the metal bars and mangled the cage. It looked like it had been hit by a serious truck. 'I'm putting this in the shed,' he said, 'so we can be reminded of what the bear is capable of.' Needless to say, we didn't' have a bird feeder after that."

"But you don't still have problems with bears now, do you?" Kathy asked, sipping at her Coke.

"Are you kidding? I'm getting to that. About twenty years later, my dad had a stroke. He couldn't talk almost at all. I hadn't heard him call me by my name for ten years. We'll I had picked him up along with one of my cousins, who was about nine, and were taking them upstate for the weekend. We drove up to the driveway and there in the headlights is this HUGE black bear. I mean this animal was mammoth. So I honked my horn like crazy because they always tell you bears don't like noise and, sure enough, the bear started moving away, but he didn't go back into the woods, he just moved further up the drive towards the house. So I drove slowly and kept honking and the automatic lights on the house went on and the bear started towards the trees.

"My dad stretched his arms out on both sides and started moving them up and down slowly to show the size of the bear's ass. And that bear had an enormous ass. 'Jesus Christ!' he said, moving his arms up and down. 'Jesus Christ!'

"I was terrified. I waited until the bear was not visible and quickly took my cousin into the house. The driveway is on a slant so the passenger side of the car is uphill. My dad couldn't get out of the car himself, even though he hated to be helped. So I went around the car, opened the door and lifted him out.

"He put his arms around me, facing towards the trees, and he got this look on his face. A look of absolute fear. He started gesturing with his chin, pointed towards the trees behind me. I was afraid to look. I knew it was the bear. He kept pointing with his chin and I turned my head. There was nothing there! He laughed and laughed."

Kathy laughed.

"'Jesus Christ!' " Mike mimicked his dad's hand gesture, both arms outstretched moving up and down. "'Jesus Christ!'"

"Excuse me, you're knocking my drink over," said the passenger on Mike's left side.

"Sorry," said Mike. "Jesus Christ."

24 E & F

"Honey, did you remember to put the garage door opener in the kitchen?"

"Hmmmmm."

"And you gave the kids our flight information? You know Susan always worries."

"Hmmmmm."

"Do you think it was a good idea to get sandwiches ahead of time? I mean it was a good idea, wasn't it?"

"Hmmmmm."

"You don't think it's extravagant for us to fly instead of taking the car?"

"Hmmmmm."

"You know, we're not getting any younger and the amount we save, what with the gas prices, and the wear and tear on our health, and what if, god forbid, the car should break down? Or we should get into an accident in some state where we have to wait for hours for the police, or the AAA, if they even have AAA?"

"Hmmmmm."

"I mean it was the right decision?"

"Hmmmmm."

"I mean, I'm not going to drive. I don't care what you say and if you got tired we would just have to pull over to the side of the road and go to sleep. Because I'm not driving on highways in god knows what godforsaken state with the speed limits of 100 miles an hour and the heat like Death Valley. Do you know how many people die just going through that part of the country in a car? I mean we could save just that much by not dying and not having to have our dead bodies flown back for the funeral. That cost alone would be twice what this plane trip is costing us. And we would have to fly that way, too, in the coffins that is, anyhow. Am I right?"

"Honey, you can't drive a car from New York to the Bahamas."

"So I'm right?"

"Hmmmmmm."

16 D & E

"I don't know why you didn't make sure of the time of the ceremony."

"That's you, always got to find a problem."

"Joseph, everything has to be perfect. Our only daughter! Lying dead 1,000 miles away!"

"You don't have to remind me! I know she's dead! I'm the one who got the phone call!"

"If only you hadn't been so cheap."

"Oh, now it's my fault. Was it my fault that she quit her job and lost her health insurance? Was it my fault that she got a better paying job?"

"She only took the new job because it paid better. Then she had a three month period before the new health insurance went into effect. If she had only had the cancer screening sooner. She would have known and we could have—"

"Come on, Mira, stop with the tears. It's not like it's a surprise. We knew she had the cancer as soon as she found out. It's just been a matter of time. Still, when the call came—It was a shock. I felt like my heart stopped beating for at least three minutes."

"And I didn't feel anything? I saw your face and I just knew, I knew! Oh!"

"Come on, now, have a little soda or something. You don't want everybody in the plane to know our business. Scotch for me, ginger ale for my wife," he said as he counted out the bills for the stewardess.

"Corn chips?" she asked.

He nodded yes and took the two packages.

"There, don't you feel a little better? The tears aren't going to help Diana."

"Maybe they help me! The doctor said I have to let out my emotions."

"Always with the doctor. The doctor this, the doctor that. I don't see this headshrinker paying for the plane tickets. Or the funeral. The doctor is just happy that you let out your emotions in his office so he can collect his big fat fee."

"What are you complaining about? I pay for it myself! I have my own money! I always have!"

"Let's just stop fighting now. Try to get some sleep. We'll be there soon enough and we're going to need all our strength. Think of Diana."

"I am thinking of her!" She took the napkin he offered and blew her nose again. She settled back in her seat.

"I only took on the extra job," he continued, " because I know we're going to need the money now, more than ever. What with your parents in the nursing home and the business going down the tubes."

" You'd think that there would always be a steady flow of customers. People have been with us for as long as we're open, 25 years."

"It's all the new fabrics; they go right in the washer, they don't need the dry cleaning."

"And they are murder to shorten. All the women who come for alterations, I can't make the knitted fabric stand still long enough to put a pin it in. And they're so heavy."

"Yeah, they sell them for travel. You try to fill a suitcase with that acetate stuff. You won't be able to lift it. But we've got to do a good job; we need this money."

"I know, Joseph, I know. You don't have to keep telling me. Didn't I suggest to put in the ads for the alterations? And to give 25% off alterations with every dry cleaning order?"

"Yes, Mira, and that was a great idea, I must admit. Keep on having ideas like that and we won't need to take on outside work. Now just get some rest."

28 B & C

"She wants to be a witch."

"Do you mean for Halloween?"

"No, she sees it as a 'calling'. She says she had a vision and now she knows what her path is."

"For goodness sake."

"Yes. And how she expects to pay the rent with this I have no idea. She has a friend, Judy, who has a little shop in town. Perhaps you've seen it? It's called 'The Wicca Wold'—they don't call themselves witches. It's Wicca and it's a religion."

"Is that the place that has all those herbs? And the crystal ball in the window with the purple drapes?"

"Yep. I think she expects to tell fortunes although why anyone would pay her $25 to lay out a bunch of cards and do her mumbo jumbo I have no idea. And she wants to change her name."

"For goodness sake."

"Yes, we're not supposed to call her Nancy anymore; we're supposed to call her Goddess of the Mandrake Wold."

"Goddess of the Man Rake Word?"

"No, Mandrake Wold; wold is another word for wood."

"That goes along with the purple nail polish and black lipstick I suppose."

"I suppose. The thing is she wouldn't be an unattractive girl if she didn't try to make herself into this Gothic novel. And the friend, Judy, she is so fat. I have a feeling she does this witchcraft thing because she can't get a boyfriend. It's this form of saying you have magic powers outside the normal realm."

"I know what you mean. You don't see these attractive girls, the kind on the step climber videos on the television, the 'after' videos, not the before. You don't see them all decked out in long droopy dresses, all dumpy and drab."

"And, of course, she thinks that it's just because I'm close minded. It never could occur to her that we had something like that in our time, but we all had long hair and wrote poetry and went to coffee houses. Listening to music our parents hated. But at least we had some kind of political orientation. I can't figure what these wiccas are going to do with themselves, except fleece the non-wiccas out of the $25 for a fortunetelling session and all kinds of expensive herbs and charms."

"I don't know, Lucy. I mean in Louisiana they have that voodoo. And the dolls that you stick pins in. And there's a whole religion, Santeria, I think it's called. People take it very seriously."

"Well, I hope Nancy doesn't intend to go around sacrificing chickens in our basement. I'll have something to say about that for sure."

"Here she comes, Lucy. Pretend we've been talking about weather in the Bahamas."

28 D & 28 C

"Hello, Aunt Ethel."

"Hello, Nancy. Your mother has just been telling me about your new name and your profession."

"Ethel!" said Mrs. Wardhope.

"I'm sorry, Lucy, but it never does to sweep things under the rug. What made you decide to be a witch?"

"It's not a witch, Aunt Ethel. It's Wicca. It's a religion, just like Hinduism or being a Presbyterian."

"I don't recall seeing any Wicca Churches in town, Nancy."

"That's because we have our own sacred spaces, to avoid the publicity and mistrust of the ignorant ones."

"Well, Nancy, if you go about hiding things of course everyone is going to think badly of you. They might think you're terrorists."

"Well, Aunt Ethel, maybe we should be terrorists."

"Nancy!"

"No, really, Mother. What with all the ignorance and prejudice today, it's amazing that anyone still believes in the good old US of A."

"Nancy, you don't really mean that!"

"Well, the United States was founded on freedom of religion and now look what we've become. Religion is only free if you believe one of the accepted faiths. Everything else is suspect. Thomas Jefferson said that we should have a revolution every five years to keep the democracy healthy. And maybe we should just do that."

"And the Bible says that the devil can quote scripture for his purpose."

"Well, at least he can read, which his more than some of the so called red blooded Americans can do."

"Nancy!"

"Mother! Don't pretend everything is fine! I know you and Daddy are suffering economically as are most of the rest of the country. Do you think that it's a democracy when 99% if the wealth is controlled by one percent of the population?"

"What does this have to do with religion?"

"I'm not sure, Ethel, I guess it all figures into the mix somehow. The point is that everything isn't fine. And we have to try new ways to make the world a place for the next generations to grow up."

"And you think that by painting your nails purple and using black lipstick this will solve things?"

"It's a start."

"And the people that blow up buildings, is that a start, too?"

"Yes, it is. I sometimes wish that I had blown up the Twin Towers myself."

"Nancy! You watch your mouth!"

19 A

I just wanna play my video game. I just wanna play my video game. I just wanna score higher and higher and higher and higher.

I just wanna hear the little beep beep beep. That's it, beep beep beep. And more and more and more!

That's it! Now I'm going strong. More than before. Higher score! Higher score! Higher score!

"Stop that, Jonquil! You give that back to me. You give that back or you'll be sorry. You'll be so sorry. There, what did I tell you? Now I've got Blue Bunny and you're not going to get him back! So there!"

19 A & B, 20 A & B

"Jonquil, now stop hitting your brother."

"But, Mommy, he stole Bunny Blue!"

"Jesse, you give your sister back her Bunny Blue."

"Bunny Blue is a stupid name. Call it Painted Rodent. Just a Blue Rat!"

"Is not! Is not!"

"Is too, is too!"

"Is not!"

"Jesse, stop hitting your sister with Bunny Blue. I don't care if it's a rodent or not. Give that to me."

"Never! I'll punch a hole in the plane and throw it down! Watch it drown!"

"You can't drown in air, Jesse. Give me the bunny. Bill, will you give me a hand here!"

"Huh?"

"Bill, take some responsibility for your son. Take Bunny Blue and— no! Don't tear it's ear off! Bill!'

"Sorry, Honey, it just kind of happened. He still looks okay, doesn't he? And look, Jonquil, the bunny has such long ears he only needs one."

"Awwwwwhhh! My Bunny Blue is going to die! Ahhwwwwh!"

"Jonquil, don't cry now, baby. Jesse, you apologize to your sister."

"Will not!"

"Will too. Bill, you make him apologize."

"Jesse, now tell your sister you're sorry. Go ahead."

"I'm sorry your stupid Bunny Blue is such a loser that he only has one ear and is going to bleed to death! So there!"

"Awwwhhhh, Mommy!"

"There, there, sweetie, Jesse didn't mean it. He's just jealous because he loves Bunny Blue so much. Tell her, Jesse, tell her."

"I won't tell her, I won't! Stop twisting my arm! Daddy, make her stop twisting my arm! Aww! That hurts!"

"Jesse, shut up. Imagine you had your ears torn off. And be thankful it's not worse."

28 F

They never should have fired me. Just the idea of it. When I started my career in TV I made sure to mistake proof my job so that I wouldn't run that risk. I mean, the reason I went that route to begin with was that the chances of getting fired were zero to none.

I'm British, I'm male, I'm handsome. Starting as a substitute for the girl who did the sports reports in the Midwest for god's sake, I was a shoe-in. The first few times she was out and I was in, the station got so many call-ins about me. And then I was promoted. And then promoted again.

Soon I was working in TV sales. American women are suckers for an English accent. All I have to do is open my mouth and they open their purses. And their legs. Well, maybe that was the problem. But I don't think so. Lots of the other show hosts fool around big time, bigger than me, and they didn't get fired.

I should have seen it coming. But how was that possible? I had been on that station for 12 years. 12 bloody years! I was chums with the right people, I dressed smartly (I've always dressed smartly). Maybe that was it, I dressed too smartly. Maybe I made the others jealous. After all, how many of them could wear a shirt with cufflinks, open at the neck, with a gold chain under it without looking like the New Jersey Mafia? I mean, come on! And my shoes! My feet are so elegant I can wear even those horrible sports shoes you have to wear with your jeans and I still look put together.

Always a blazer with the jeans, always clean shaven. None of that five o'clock shadow that you see on the action shows. Like it's really possible that a man will have exactly the same amount of shadow every time they film him. Whether it's 10 AM or 6 PM, the man always looks the same. Who would believe that? But then again, who would believe that every single piece of trumped up jewelry we are selling is going to become a family heirloom to be passed down the line to every daughter until they are sick of looking at it? "Look, here's Helen again wearing the cameo pendant that was tasteless 50 years ago but a gift from her mum." I mean, come on. Get bloody real.

And still they fired me! Well, I showed them. I didn't take that lying down, no bloody way. And I didn't call any lawyer or any union rep. No, I took action. I took a stand. Come Monday morning they'll know that they can't push Helmut Hardcastle, the housewives' darling, around anymore. Just watch the looks on their faces. I wish I were there to see it, but I can't risk that. Oh, no. It'll really knock their socks off, and more than just their socks.

"Yes, a nice white wine, please. On second thought, do you have champagne? I'm having a little celebration, just me, myself, and I."

8 A

"Everything could have been foretold. It was exactly like knowing the house always wins or the new car will always get a dent. Or that which you underestimate will end up saving your skin.

"The willow tree waved its branches in the gentle wind. The water was green. The fir trees she had seen grow up for five years were now flourishing. Two herons crossed the stream, flying. Three canoes paddled around the corner of the stream.

"It was a tranquil setting, this window on the stream, and she enjoyed this brief space of relaxation because she sensed that what was coming would require all the strength she had saved up. And then some."

"Excuse me, madam, would you like something to drink?" asked the handsome flight attendant. Or at least Enid Snark thought he was handsome. When you get over the age of 80 any young man looks handsome.

"Yes, I would like a ginger ale with ice, please." She closed her laptop briefly and gazed up at him, expecting that there might be a charge. Everyone was talking about all the new charges on planes, you never could tell.

"And some nuts?" he asked as he put the plastic glass of ginger ale in front of her. She nodded.

It was good to take a break from the new novel. Now that she was older there were fewer distractions, especially when she was at home. When she was younger she used to love to write on airplanes; she felt detached from everything, above it all, very literally and also metaphorically. Now she was used to travel; the book signings in different cities were really fun. She had never imagined that she would become so successful or that it would be so easy and painless.

She took a sip of the ginger ale and got back to her work. She was going to have to throw some suspense into this one. Too much poetry and you lost the reader. They were used to all this action and violence.

She smiled to herself. She had tried a little experiment, something to see if one of her plot ideas would actually be possible in real life. Maybe it was wicked of her, but she didn't seriously believe that any harm would come of it.

"People are too sophisticated to be taken in so easily," she thought to herself. She would just sit back and watch it all unwind.

She took another sip of ginger ale and began to type.

17 D again

Well, forget that trying to close my eyes. I don't know why every little thing is a great big fuss on a plane. It's like having your neighbors right in the middle of your living room. Although, sometimes that might not be such a bad idea.

When I lived on the East Side there was a chick living next door, a real looker. Come to think of it, she was a flight attendant, or stewardess as they called them way back. She was in and out of her pad all hours with all kinds of guys coming in and out.

Once she came over to see if I had some ginger ale. She was wearing this next to nothing black baby doll night gown. And she knew how to work it. Next time I was home alone and heard no sounds from her place I rang the bell. There she was in an oversized t-shirt and those long legs.

"Thought you might want some company," I said. "After all, we are neighbors."

She knew what I wanted right away. "How neighborly of you, " she said.

"I guess you girls get all kinds of freebees on the flights," I started. "How about a little something to powder your nose?" She smiled again.

We went through a pile of my best stuff and soon we were drinking and getting it on right on the sofa. Old Mack used to say, "Put the flag over her head and fuck her for Old Glory." That was about it. And then some.

Man, this is getting me too tense. I wish that girl of Sport's would make a sign. If it were that neighbor of mine, she didn't need to be asked twice. I should get points for trying to be friendly.

Hey, I can't take this suspense or maybe I just deserve a reward. Into the bathroom

I will go, I will go, I will go.

"Excuse me." Sorry to trip over your big fat feet, you old gink, but Sunny needs to powder his nose.

There we go, lock the door, take out the stash. Surprised I got by the dogs? Not really, there were no dogs! I would have ditched it in the men's room in the airport if I felt a sniff was coming my way.

Open up the paper. Hey! The plane just hit an air pocket. Now the coke is all over me. Wow, I'd better snort all I can and just flush the rest down the toilet.

Lucky there are no sniffing dogs on this plane. Well, I did see that one chick back there with a pooch but he's too tiny to have much of a nose.

Hey, easy does it, Sunny. Easy does it. Wow, the inside of my nose must look like the Holland Tunnel in a snow storm.

Wow, the top of my head is out of this plane. I can't take anymore. Put it on my gums. Swallow some. If I don't it will go to waste. Open up the old schnozola —

I could throw up. I need a soda, a ginger ale. Some sugar. I need a menthol—too bad we can't

smoke. My heart is going out of my rib cage. Can't breathe. Can't stand. Standing—grasp the door

handle.

I almost forgot to dust off my pants. I look like the Abominable Snowman with dandruff.

21 A & B again

"Karen, wake up.   I want to use the restroom."

"I wasn't sleeping. And I thought you didn't have to go."

"That was before; this is now."

"Can you get up out of the seat, Livy?"

"If they can make it up to the top of Everest, I can get up out of an airplane seat."

"Well, prepare to navigate through the aisle. Hold on to the seat backs."

"Don't tell me how to walk; I've been doing it for decades."

"I'll come with you."

"Excuse me, I don't mean to knock into you."

"(She's 92 years old, my mom.)"

"Isn't that wonderful. She's so sweet."

Smile. "Yes, she seems very loveable. Do you want an extra mother? I can rent her cheap."

"You shouldn't talk about your mother that way. I wish my mom were still with me."

"Karen, I thought you were coming."

"Right behind you, Mom. Do you want me to pick up one of those magazine on the way back?"

"Why bother. I've read it all before. Same words, just a different order."

"You might like the pictures."

"And you might like my foot in your behind. Wouldn't you know—occupied."

"Guess you're not the only one who wants to use the restroom."

"Hey, come on! People are waiting!"

"Livy, you can't just force your way—It's not polite."

" Don't tell me what I can or can't do. I once stood in the middle of Sixth Avenue waiting for the lights to change with the cars streaming all around me. Hurry it up, hurry it up! Well, finally. Hold my coat."

"Give me the coat. I'll be right here."

"Don't rush me; it's not polite."

21 A & B, 17 D, 26A

"Hey, watch it lady. What do you think you're doing?"

"I'm 92 years old. I'm at the door of a restroom. What do you think, I'm playing canasta?"

"You could have your nose broken if you don't watch out."

"That's no way to talk to your elders, young man."

"You want to make something of it?"

"I'd quit, sonny, while you're ahead, if I were you."

"Who asked you to butt in? Are you the Emperor of the Airways or something?"

"If you have to ask you can't be told so just sit down and shut up or I'll sit you down myself."

"Oh, Mr. Big Man on Campus. How are you going to look with your teeth all over your sports coat?"

"You don't' want to start what you can't finish—"

"Please, please. Mom, just go into the restroom. there's no point in making a big deal of this. I appreciate what you're trying to do, Mr. — —————?"

"Mr. Talenkov, at your service."

"Mr. Talenkov. My mom's okay. Aren't you, Mom?"

"Are you kidding? Two handsome men fighting over me? If I knew this was what riding in a plane was like I would have booked a flight years ago."

Caleb Jameson, custodial engineer, airport terminal

I don't know what these people expect—that you can clean the floor without them moving their feet and their luggage. It's not enough that I am invisible, but that my actions should also be invisible, like an automatic buff 'n shine while they drink their high priced cappuccino and wait for their flight to take off.

Years ago it was easier; people still cleaned up some of their own houses and had respect for someone doing the job they did at home. Now everyone can afford a flight to the Tropical Paradise and they want to be pampered all the way from the terminal on this end to the terminal on the other side.

For a while, yes, there were problems with the terrorists in the airplanes and everyone was too distracted by that to worry about my mop getting close to their luggage. I think now they'd like it better if I were one of those zumba machines that goes by remote control and cleans until it hits the wall. Just wait until I hit the wall; I won't just stand there and rev my wheels.

"Excuse me, madam. That's right, just move the suitcase over a little. Thank you." Now why can't everyone be like this lady? Minimum of effort, easy does it.

Let me just get under the table here. How they leave all the straw wrappers. And the stirring sticks. You'd think there were no clearly marked receptacles for the different types of garbage.

But sometimes you find something surprising. I remember finding that cute little puppy in a suitcase that wouldn't close. They said it was a dangerous breed when I brought it into the office. Looked so lost and cute to me. And apparently to the supervisor who took it home, claimed it was worth over $800.

And the restrooms! Don't get me started. I wonder if they leave their houses with the same mess they leave here.

Now I'll just get around the corner of this trash can and into the gift shop space.

Hey! What's this? Not a suitcase, but a brown paper wrapped package inside an open knapsack. Looks like it might be something I don't want to go touching. Looks like what they show us in the videos about bombs in the terminal.

"Hey! Sir! Don't go near that!"

I'd better call on the cell. "Mr. Thompson, I think we have a problem here. A package in a knapsack like the ones on the instruction video." Pause. "Yes, I'll just wait here." Pause. "Oh, you'll put some security personnel on it and clear that part of the terminal? Good. Shame it's near the gift shop. I'll put orange cones around the area and a CLOSED sign."

I wonder if they're going to delay the flights now. I wonder if the person who left it is here. If it were me, I'd be long gone.

30 D

Is this finally my seat?Not too far from the restroom and on the aisle, praise the Lord. Looks like the plane is full. Many souls seeking a path to righteousness but how many will find it? Many are called but few are chosen. Many are called. You remember that, Ethiopia, you remember that.

So many with the trappings of wealth dripping from their fingers. Gold watches, golden rings. Look at that man there with dungarees and dirty hair, but he's got to have his gold Rolex and the diamond stud in the ear. No Golden Calf for me. My treasure is stored up in Heaven. And the Lord has showed me the way, praise the Lord.

And that girl on the aisle. All that turquoise Indian jewelry. She doesn't look Native American, but maybe I'm wrong. So hard to tell these days. And impossible to judge. Only the One Lord and Savior who I chose to call Jesus, my personal savior, can do that.

Oh, should I have a beverage? Well, a glass of cider might not be out of place. Or maybe a glass of wine? Take a little wine for thy stomach's sake. Yes, this flight certainly is a celebration and a glass of wine, for celebratory purposes, would not be construed amiss.

"Thank you, the red wine, please. Thank you."

She certainly looks very pleased with herself. I wonder if she is just another agent of Satan. So many of these flight attendants, going back and forth, sleeping in a strange place every night, have the opportunity to sin. And it takes a strong soul to resist temptation. Yes, Lord, that's something I know from personal trials. I have been tempted, yes, I have. And I have resisted, not through my own strength but with the help of the Almighty.

"Excuse me, Madam, do you think I could have another glass of the red wine? Yes, thank you."

Now look at her, looking at me, judging me. Judge not lest you shall be judged. My body is larger and therefore I can drink more and not become intoxicated. But I don't think that would occur to a hussy like her. Blonde haired, and not natural, I imagine.

And that male attendant, smiling at her. I imagine he has sins of his own. Here he goes down the aisle rubbing up against people's arms and legs, doubtless getting pleasure from the contact. And to think these sinners are in charge of our comfort! Well, at least they're not in charge of our salvation.

Only one that has that responsibility is Our Lord and Savior who I chose to call Jesus Christ. Blessed be those who hunger and thirst for righteousness for they shall be satisfied. Yes, blessed be. I can drink to that.

"Sir, another glass of the red, please."

16 D

Here I am, praise Allah, getting through the security and all the checking. And here I will carry out my purpose, praise Allah.

It's enough these ignorant people don't know what is happening right under their noses. It's enough they look at me and judge me just by the way I look. Well, maybe that's for the best. They think I'm a terrorist and so they take extra care.

Look at the way they pulled me out of line and delayed me and my baggage as everyone else was boarding. And all the questions, the searching. They could not even spell my name correctly! No wonder they could not find anything in their computer. All totally expected. And dealt with successfully.

No doubt, I have to be prepared for all this suspicion. Which is not true for the others. Any one of them could be a terrorist, but because they are not people of color they can go through the security without being stopped.

But I kept my temper, praise Allah. I did not make any remarks to the security personnel, although I was very tempted. It does no good to fight this discrimination. You must be prepared for it and endure it calmly. It is a test of the will of Allah. A test which I passed.

And now I can go on to fulfill my greater purpose, Allah be praised.

7 F

I can't believe I'm finally getting to take a trip. Always it was the family this, the family that. Now it's just me. And I'm not going to think it's "The End of Life Café" for me. No, I've still got time ahead of me.

No one knows how much. No one really knows very much in life actually at all. Of course you always THINK YOU KNOW. You pay your electric bill because you don't want them to turn off the electricity; you don't think that maybe the house will burn down and there'll be no more need for your TV or your toaster. You pay your medical insurance because you think it will save you money in the long run; you don't think that you'll get hit by a truck, drop dead and have paid for a month you didn't need.

You know, sometimes I think the people in the Middle Ages had it better than we do now. They had the Bubonic plague which could kill you in a day. You'd wake up in the morning and you'd be fine and then by the evening, boom! Your throat would swell up, you'd turn purple and start to bloat. Ready to be carted off to the cemetery.

And they thought it was a judgment from God, who would live and who would die. They didn't know that the fleas carried it. And the fleas were carried on the backs of the rats which lived in the straw that they used for bedding. So they would move to another city to avoid the plague but they'd take their bedding with them. So the fleas would be in the bedding and they would take the plague to a new city.

That was where the saying "Carpe Diem" came from: seize the day. Enjoy it while you can because you never know how much time you have left.

So the people in the Middle Ages would kick up their heels and enjoy the day because it might just be their last.

Maybe the people on this plane should do the same. After all, none of them even thinks that this might be the last flight they'll ever take.

Maybe they shouldn't take so much for granted.

11 F

I can't believe I finally did it. Takes a lot of arranging to be able to get away. All those patients, "Dr. Lee, how long will you be gone?" "Dr. Lee, I don't know how I'll be able to go a week and a half without an appointment." Maybe they should try going for a year and a half solid without a break, except for holidays and holiday weekends. I need to get away.

Not that I don't love my patients. Hey! Here I am on my first vacation in almost two years and I'm thinking about the office. Wendy, cut it out!

"Stewardess, could I have a vodka tonic, please." Now that's more like it.

"Peanuts?"

"Not really," Wendy said.

"We have other snacks, like these gluten free crackers which are very tasty."

"Sure, why not?" I'll live it up for a change. As long as I don't eat a couple of bags full I'll be all right. Well, maybe I should just save them for the hotel. After all, if something goes wrong and we get delayed it could be hours before I get to eat anything real.

"Thank you, Doctor," said Cynthia.

"How do you know I'm a doctor?" Wendy asked.

"We make it our business to keep track. In case there's an emergency. Not that we're expecting any trouble," Cynthia was quick to add.

"Good," Wendy nodded.

"Do you mind me asking what your specialty is?" Cynthia took her money for the vodka tonic.

"I'm an acupuncturist," Wendy smiled. She waited for the normal reaction of either ignorance or shock.

"Wow!" Cynthia exclaimed. "My mom goes to acupuncture! Ever since her arthritis got really bad. She can't do without it."

Just what I wanted to hear, thought Wendy. "That's good," she said. "I'm glad it can help her."

"I think acupuncture is just great," Cynthia continued. "Once when I was on a flight to China I stayed over and did some travelling. I saw a man have his appendix removed without any anesthetic except for acupuncture. It was amazing."

"Yes," said Dr. Lee. Here was someone who was not as ignorant as she might at first appear. "There are many things that acupuncture can do; most people just think we stick needles in people, like hypodermics."

Cynthia laughed. "I know," she said. "Like most people think that stewardesses are the big go-go girls of the air. Like our life is one big non-stop party."

Dr. Lee smiled. "Well you certainly are cheerful enough to enjoy every minute."

Cynthia smiled. "Thank you, Doctor." She gave her an extra bag of gluten free crackers.

16 A & B

"There, honey, you just settle yourself. No one is going to bother you, my sweetie, you are my one and only Therapy Dog and you travel right along with Mama, there, there."

I wish this plane ride didn't cost so much money; then I could cut down on the expenses. But if I didn't take the plane I couldn't get the job done. Oh, well. That's the way of it.

That last shrink certainly cost me the proverbial arm and a leg. I remember when I asked him how psychiatrists refer to their patients.

"One brick short of a load, several spots missing on their dice, not the brightest crayon in the box, his elevator doesn't go all the way to the top, a candidate for the Laughing Academy, another one for the Funny Farm? Or just plain crazy," he laughed.

Like he ever knew how tough it is to have a terminal illness. I'd like him to have three days of what I go through and then see how he changes his tune.

"Isn't that so, Doggo? Mommy's good little dog."

WOOF, WOOF, WOOF, WAG, WAG, another treat, WAG, WAG.

And the money the medication costs. I could have bought a great car, scratch that, a motor home. A deluxe motor home! And still have money left for gasoline. And that's saying something.

Well, no point in stressing. If all goes as planned we'll soon be rolling in clover, "Won't we, Doggo?"

WAG, WAG, WOOF, pant pant pant, Scratch head.

I can't believe how easy it is. I mean with all the publicity you'd think that they would take more precautions, at least at the airport. But, hey, I'm not complaining, it just makes my job easier.

And when you've got nothing, you've got nothing to lose. No pain, no gain. No, let's not go there. There isn't going to be any pain in this at all. Not like there was before.

I remember when Dave left. I didn't even know he was going to leave. They just took him away. I think they thought I was a bad influence on him. As if anyone could influence Dave . I thought it didn't bother me and then later that day when I was at work I remember I was standing in the middle of Second Avenue. And I just started to cry. And I kept crying all day. I couldn't stop. I was all alone and nothing mattered but Dave. I don't know why. I think it was knowing that something, some important part of my life had gone and was never coming back. It would never be the same. I know that sounds trite. I mean every day is different and every day will never be the same as any other day, but them taking him away like that. And I just couldn't stop crying.

But this is going to be different. A nice clean getaway with no complications. I knew what I was getting myself in for and now all we have to do is relax and enjoy the ride. "Isn't that so, Doggo? Isn't that so, my little precious?" How you just keep licking and licking!

WAG, WAG, Scratch, scatch, LICK, LICK.

I mean, it's like they never suspect the lady with the baby. So visible I'm invisible. Nothing to it but to do it, "Right, Doggo? Right, honey?"

LICK, LICK, LICK, WAG, WAG, scratching, scratching, WOOF.

26 A again

Thank goodness for Homeland Security. All that airport checking, nothing gets on the plane. I don't have to worry about my equipment. Either I bring one of my home growns in the baggage or just put something together once I get there. No hurry no worry.

Can't say I'm enthusiastic about this next hit. From what they already told me, it's like so many little fish, not worth bothering over. That means it's easy to get sloppy. I must overcome this feeling of false security. But then that's what I'm known for: rising to the occasion. And demolishing the occasion.

That little punk back at the restroom could have caused quite a problem. I'm just a sucker for little old ladies—reminds me of my mom.

"Stewardess! Hey! Jack on the rocks! Here, sweetie, here's a little something for you." They like when I tuck it in their uniform. Especially the ones getting older. A woman's never too old to flirt. Learned that from my mom. 80 if she was a day and always complaining, "The worst thing about getting old is that there are no more men out there!"

Glad that she didn't live to see this. Not that I'm not doing alright, not by a long shot. Apartment in any city I choose, nice cars, nice clothes, nice women. But Mom always hoped that I would settle down and she'd be a grandma. Well, no profession is perfect. When you have to be invisible, you can't put down too many roots. I'm stretching it as is.

That last job was pretty hairy. Hope this one is a little smoother. Keeps you on your toes and I don't do all that training with the equipment for nothing. Good physique for a man my age, for a man any age. Full head of hair, all mine, even avoided having an ulcer. Too many in my line of work let the stress get to them.

My secret? You only live once and the more people you get to first makes your life easier and longer. Ice the next guy before he ices you. Too many damn people in the world. And not enough turtles. Turtles have the right idea: protection no matter where you go. No shark is going to eat a turtle, no octopus can strangle them. And the teeth on the snapping turtle. Wowee! Get that thing biting you and you'll lose a hand or a foot.

The Native Americans believe that the Earth is riding on the back of a gigantic tortoise. I read this old lady in England was at a lecture of one of those physics guys who was telling about the origin of the world.

She raised her hand. "Young man, the Earth is a riding on the back of a giant tortoise," she said.

"And what," asked the clever lecturer, "is the tortoise resting on?"

"You may think you're very smart," she replied, "but it's turtles all the way down!" What guts. The old geezers have it. They've lived long enough to have escaped most of their natural predators. If they watch their health and don't let anything or anyone get to them, they've got it made.

Unlike my next assignment who is going to take a long walk on a short pier, as the saying goes. Or something like that.

31 F

Test file.   Open.   Check for the numbers.   Correct.   Save.

Test file. Open.   Check for correct headings.   Correct.   Save.

Test file.   Open.   Check for correct statistics.   Correct.   Save.

File.   Correct order.   Save.

File.   Correct order.   Save.

SNACK. SNACK.   Drink alcohol.

No movie.

Read MY MAGAZINE.   Photo ads color ads send away ads article article .

I've read this before.

Sleep.   hohohohoho.   Gottcha.

31 F again

I am flying at the top of the room. I go into room after room and the doors open for me. I don't touch the ceiling, but I have to watch my head.

I am going to the health club in the city. I have my dog with me and there's a check-out girl who takes the dog and gives me a number. I will tip her on the way out. I am awkward and make a mistake and tip her on the way in. She looks at me funny. I explain I will also tip her on the way out. I finish my work out and go home when I realize I've forgotten the dog.

I go back but first I have to close the doors of the canteen where the boss is relaxing. They are expecting others to arrive and I don't want them disturbed.

25 A & B again

""Did I say something wrong? You look a little distant. I'm sorry, I don't mean to be prying."

"It's not you," said Frank. "I had to put my dog to sleep yesterday."

"I'm so sorry."

"I know it was the best thing. She was suffering. Lymphoma."

"How old was she?"

"Twelve."

"That's a long time."

"Yeah."

"My dog Jones, when he died I would walk the trails I went on with him every day. And I would bring back a stone and place it on his grave. After a while I was wearing away the dirt around the grave and I knew: it was time for another dog. I went to the SPCA and got Brandy.

"I feel that Brandy was sent to me by Jones. I used to fight a lot with my mom. After Jones died I dreamed he came to me and told me, 'Don't fight with each other.' Brandy gets upset and barks when we fight, so we've had to stop."

16 D & E again, 16 A & B again

"Joseph, there's no use torturing yourself."

"It's not torture, Mira. This is our daughter we're burying."

"But looking at the photos over and over—"

"I'm trying to decide which ones will go best in front of the funeral parlor."

"We can decide that later."

"We always say, 'We can do it later'. Well, for Diana there is no more later. We have to do it now."

"You dropped one. Here, I'll get it. Oh, that dog –"

"I'm so sorry. Here, Doggo give it back. There, he doesn't know what he's doing. I hope he didn't hurt the picture."

"Give me that."

"Joseph, she's trying to help. Now, see, we'll just smooth it out a little. Good as new."

"She's a beautiful girl. Is that your daughter?"

"Yes, she just died. We're going to bring her back for the funeral."

"I'm so sorry. I didn't know."

"These are pictures for the memorial."

"She was a beautiful girl."

"Thank you."

"Doggo, sit still. Here, is a little something I just drew." Candy opened her sketchbook and handed it to them.

"Why, Joseph, look at this. It looks just like us. You drew this?"

"Yes, it's my hobby."

"Well, you're very good. It should be more than a hobby. I should think you'd be able to make a living out of this. Joseph, take a look."

"That's very good. You've got Mira's nose just right."

"You know, if you like I could make a drawing from one of your photographs of your daughter."

"You could do that?"

"Yes. And maybe you could incorporate it into the memorial. Maybe on the program."

"Why, that would be wonderful!   Joseph, what do you think?"

"That would be all right."

"I think it's a wonderful idea. You are very kind."

"I wish I could do more."

"It's very nice of you. I wish there were more young people like you. Thank you."

21 F

Today is my day. I can feel it.

Age: the great leveler. Here I am at the age when I can afford my obvious good taste, which means dressing not very expensively, but very carefully so that anyone who sees me remarks, inwardly, "Aren't the clothes and accessories she has chosen in exceptional good taste? Where did she get them?" Objects collected over the years of not being able to get the standard expensive items, but picking things unusual and unique to me. This makes me ambitious and confident.

I remember when I was a child and I would come home from school. My father would call me into his study.

"And how did you do in school today?" he would ask. I was terrified that somehow he had found out something, some small misbehavior which the teacher had brought to his attention. And for those moments I would wait for his pronouncement, a hug if I did well and a stern reprimand if I did not.

"Well, your teacher called and," he would pause, "you did very well in your presentation." And then would come the hug. No matter how tight he held me it never made up for the fear I felt as I wondered what his reaction would be. I made up my mind that I would never let anyone have that power over me again.

Yes, today is my day. The beginning of a new era which will astound everyone. My turn to meet out the rewards and punishments. And yet to look at me no one would guess. And that is part of the deliciousness of it.

17 D again,16 A & B

Well, now I can relax just a little. Just a little. Don't want to get over confident. That's when things can really screw up. I've got my health, well sort of. I've got plenty of dough. I've got plan A and plan B and I guess I can come up with more if I need to. Don't even think about it.

Let me just take a peek at my insurance, so to speak. My little book with all my numbers that will get me into my bank accounts, my little Fort Knoxes, my golden boxes. The breast pocket. No, I guess it's in my pants. Back pocket. No, now this is not funny anymore. Stand up, Sunny. Check carefully. Not in any pants pocket. Not in my carry on. Put all the papers on the seat. It could be hiding. Just like it to do that and scare me half to death. Not in the front zip pocket, not in the back or in the inner compartments.

Hell, they make too many pockets inside these things. Where is it? Where is it? I must have left it in the restroom when I did the coke. That's it. Go slow, don't run down the aisle like a mad man.

Occupied. Well, that's rich. Actually it could be rich if the bastard inside finds my little book. How long does it take anyhow? "Hey, are you coming out?" Take it easy, Sunny. If he has the book you'll confront him as he exits. Take it easy.

"What's your problem, man?"

"I'm sorry, did you find anything in there? I left an address book—"

"I didn't find anything. And you stop pounding on the door when people are busy. Thank you very much."

Maybe it was the other compartment. No, no, it was this one.

Here comes the stewardess.

"Stewardess, I must have misplaced my address book. It's very important. Did anyone turn in a little black book?"

"No, sir, I'm sorry. But I will be sure to be on the lookout."

"Thank you. It's very important." Great, like she could care. I'll check the other restroom anyhow.

No luck. This is getting serious. If only I memorized those numbers or wrote them down somewhere else. This is really the pits. I knew I shouldn't have done that coke. If I had my wits about me I wouldn't have lost the book. Now I am royally screwed.

Better sit down. How can I stay seated? Well, maybe the stewardess will find something. Keep calm, Sunny. Your luck has gotten you this far; just keep cool.

"Excuse me, did you drop this?"

"Yes! Thank you, thank you! You have no idea—"

"My dog found it under one of the seats."

"It must have fallen out of my pocket. Thank you, thank you, thank you. Can I buy you a drink? That's the least I can do."

"No, thank you, I'm fine."

"My name is Sunny, by the way. And you're—?"

"Candy. And this is Doggo. You can thank him too."

"Thank you, Candy, and thank you, too, Doggo. Can I pet him?"

"Yes, he's friendly. Hey, he likes you."

"At least he likes my nose. He's licking it like crazy. Hey, that's enough for now. I don't want him to get germs. But thank you both. You saved my life."

"No problem."

21 A & B again

"Karen, are they coming around with the drinks yet?"

"Livy, you can't drink with your medication, you know that."

"I know, I know, but I want a soft drink. Look; they're all up in front in the higher priced seats.

Wouldn't you think they'd have some consideration for age."

"Livy, you always say you don't want anyone to treat you differently because of your age."

"I know, but that's just what I say. I use the 92 year old bit whenever I can. Whatever works. After all, you're only 92 once."

"And next year you'll use the '93 year old' bit?"

"Hell, yes. Here's the money And remember, I want change."

"I know that. Which do you want to change first, your appearance or your attitude?"

"Karen!"

25 E & F

"Honey, tell me a story so I can fall asleep on this bumpy airplane."

"Once upon a time there was a little boy named Joe—"

"Great!"

"You say that every time. Now, my adorable husband who just happens to have the same name, this little boy also named Joe would sit all day long watching the TV and listening to videos and to DVDs. He didn't want to do anything his wife asked him to do. He didn't want to make a sign to put over the garbage so the garbage men would know where the extra bags were—"

"Ho, ho, ho."

"He didn't want to put his clothes in the plastic tubs at the foot of the bed so the heat wouldn't be blocked and the bedroom would be warm. And whenever his wife asked him to do these things he would say, 'Your mother's ass' or 'Stick it up your ass'. He had no idea how lucky he was."

"I'm regretting this already."

"Well, one day Joe fell asleep and this magic fairy came to him. The fairy took him to one of the alternative universes where things were different. In this world Joe was only three feet tall and his wife was three feet tall, but the dog was still the normal size so the dog was like a horse for little Joe. And little Joe couldn't open the refrigerator door, he couldn't drive his car to get to the movie theatre or to the mall to buy more videos and DVDs. And he was worrying about being attacked by the dog who was now a threatening size."

"Enough! Enough! I should tell you that Ellis has just written an article in <u>Scientific American</u> where he disputes the many worlds hypothesis. He worked with Stephen Hawking so he has some weight. He says there is no one to observe the many worlds so therefore it cannot exist. That's it in a nutshell."

"Well, nutshell or not, in this of the many worlds Joe was very small and very vulnerable. So he said to the fairy, 'Please take me back to my wonderful world that I never appreciated.' And the fairy did just that. And little Joe was happy to be home and to make the sign for the garbage men and to put his clothes in the plastic tubs. And he knew that in the world of dreams there are always many worlds and each of them happens at the same time and anything is possible in these many worlds. And he knew that he was lucky to be in his world. And they lived happily ever after. Amen."

6 A, B & C

"Well, Jerry, what do you want to do when we get to Nassau?"

"You mean after we transfer this sorry sack of bones at the terminal?"

"Exactamundo. I feature getting a nice steak dinner and maybe seeing the aquarium. I hear it's really nice."

"I never figured you for a fish nut."

"Live and learn."

"And what if we don't get to turn him right over? Is he coming for dinner and the aquarium with us? Hey, Mister Speak No Evil, you like to watch the fish?"

"Hey, Jerry, maybe he likes seeing the fish as long as he isn't sleeping with them!"

"Hohoho, you are so funny I forgot to laugh."

"What's that noise? You, stay put."

"He's got the cuffs on him. I'll stay with him, you go check it out."

Billy Bronze, co-pilot

Well, it's another flight with good ol' Herb "Be Right" Stark. Can't say I'm surprised. Sometimes I feel I'm the only guy that doesn't complain about flying with the old coot. He looks okay, to the unpracticed eye. But to me, I can tell the signs of fraying around the edge.

First it's taking a drink at the airport before takeoff. Then it's taking another drink in the men's room. And sneaking a bottle in your flight bag. Well, Herb isn't one to hit the booze too much, I'll say that for him. I mean, after a close call he'll take a belt, but he's not one to get carried away in that obvious a manner.

No, it's the iron clad insistence on Being Right all the time. It was bad enough before he got the nickname. After that he was near insufferable. At least to those of us under his command. He'd joke about it, sure, but he was very, very touchy whenever he felt his orders were being questioned. Even when it was just about something so simple as having to take another runway on takeoff. I mean, come on! There's things that are not worth getting upset over.

I should know. I've had a tough time of it as far back as I can remember. And the only thing that kept me sane was being FLEXIBLE. Better bend than break, my dad always used to say. And with old Herb in command I've had plenty of experience, let me tell you.

When the wife didn't want me to spend so much time away from home, I just said, "Yes, dear," and tried to rearrange my schedule as best I could. I wasn't always successful, but she knew I gave it my best shot. And when they needed me to take an extra flight because someone else was sick or unavailable, at the last minute, I always said, "Yes, sir," and didn't make a big deal of it.

That's probably why I got stuck with old Be Right Herb again. Other co-pilots try to arrange it so they're not on his route, just so they won't have to laugh at his jokes and keep nodding, "Yes, Herb, no, Herb." I have to give it to him, though, that he manages to pull the plane out of some tough spots. When the chips are down Ol' Be Right comes through.

That's why I can put other concerns aside and be his second in command. I know that at the end of the day I'll be safe and sound and coming home to the little woman. Maybe I'm getting a little too set in my ways to enjoy the suspense of a dangerous landing, or a stretch of bad weather.

Time to stop wool gathering. Let's get this show on the road.

PART II – The events

"Hello? Yes, this is the pilot. What? Repeat that. More slowly. There was a bomb in the terminal and a message saying that there is also a bomb on the plane? Are you sure? This isn't just some kind of hoax?

"And what are we supposed to do? Where is the bomb? You don't know? Well, that certainly is helpful. What are we supposed to do now?

"Call the air marshal? Does he know what to do? Oh, they said that the bomb is in the panels in the plane? And he knows how to find it?

"Well, what if he doesn't know where it its? What if he can't find it? And are we supposed to tell the passengers? Not at first, I realize that. He will go down into the inside of the plane and search around and hopefully find this bomb.

"And who is doing this exactly? Some kind of terrorist group? No? Well, who is it then? Someone calling themselves 'The Hole in One'? What exactly is that supposed to mean? Some kind of a joke? Oh, it's a dig at corporate America? And what do they want? Or is it just a game of find the bomb and make the crew run around like crazy people?

"They didn't say what they want. Great. And what does he do when he finds this bomb? Oh, we'll get more instructions? Well, that's a comfort.

"I must say that I don't think you're handling this in the best possible way. I mean, you could have tried to pin them down a bit better. How the hell should I know what you should have said? This is your ball game, not ours. We're just the ones getting the fallout. You're not the ones who are going to be blown to bits, now are you?

"I'm sorry; I forgot about the bomb in the terminal. Was anyone hurt? Oh, just the custodial staff and seven people in the gift shop. No serious injuries. Well, that's something.

"What? I didn't hear you. Oh, they said that if we don't comply there will be more attacks? This is just the beginning? Well, I always knew we were being too soft on those terrorists. If they took sterner measures none of this would be happening now.

"Which one of the passengers is it? What do you mean 'what do I mean'? Well, there's bound to be someone on this end who is part of this fiasco. They wouldn't just put a bomb up here and count on it to go off and us to follow their instructions, would they? Or are they as disorganized as some of the people on your end?

"I'm sorry, but it's not your ass that will be blown sky high. What? They said we have an hour? So what am I doing wasting time talking to you? Same to you.

"Cynthia Billings, come to the cockpit. Cynthia Billings."

****

"Yes, Captain."

"Close the door, Cynthia. I just received a message from the terminal. There's a bomb on board. Just take a minute and calm yourself. We only have an hour. The air marshal will have to go into the body of the plane and dismantle it. They're going to send more instructions. Do you know the air marshal?"

"Yes, Henry Hackerstein."

"Do you know anything about him? Have you flown with him before?"

"Yes, Captain."

"Well, take him aside and explain the situation to him briefly. Don't let the passengers overhear you. And you'd better tell your partner, Happy Charles, but don't do it where he can panic. We have to be calm if we want to come out of this thing alive. I don't mind telling you that I think the terminal could have handled this better. We're on the hook for their mistakes,"

"Are they sure there is a bomb, sir?"

"Well, they had one go off in the terminal. Injured eight people, including custodial staff. Went off in the gift shop, they said. So I guess it is pretty serious. But don't panic. If there were nothing we could do they probably wouldn't tell us; they'd just let us blow up. Sorry, just being cynical. Go on, clock is ticking.

"And, Cynthia. I know this was to be your last flight. God willing, it won't be the last for all of us."

****

"Happy, come into in to the rest room; I have to talk with you."

"Well, Cynthia, I didn't realize you were part of the mile high club!"

"I wish it were that, Hap. Come on, keep it quiet. Now, lock the door, will you?"

"Door locked."

"The captain just called me in. There was a bomb in the terminal—"

"Good Lord! Did anyone get hurt?"

"Eight including custodial. Bomb went off in the gift shop. No serious injuries. They say there's another on the plane."

"I don't believe I'm hearing this."

"They are going to give instructions. The air marshal has to go into the body of the plane to dismantle it. We have an hour."

" Hackerstein?"

"Yes."

"Well, I pray for all our sakes he knows what he's doing. Has he ever dealt with anything like this before?"

"I don't know. Not that I am aware. They say they have demands and if we do as they say we'll be alright."

"Demands from us? What do they want? Are we supposed to fly the plane somewhere?"

"I don't know. I just know the captain asked me to talk with you and ask you to help keep the passengers calm. We don't tell them anything. Yet."

"Got you. Do you tell Hackerstein or do I?"

"I'll talk with him. Why don't you go around and see if anyone wants a blanket or some peanuts or something."

"I'll try to keep my hands from shaking. I don't mind telling you that won't be easy."

"Ditto to that."

****

Cynthia Billings went up to Harry Hackerstein's seat. He was the only passenger in that row. " Mr. Hackerstein, would you please come with me into the galley? Just act normal, don't fuss."

"Of course," he rose slowly.

When Cynthia was certain that no one was in earshot she began. "The plane has been threatened. The pilot got word a bomb was placed in the airport; eight were wounded including a custodial engineer. They say there's a bomb on this plane now and you have to go into the body of the plane to dismantle it."

There was a silence.

"I understand—" she began.

"Of course I'll do it," he said.

"They said they'd give directions." Cynthia was silent. This was not exactly in her job description.

"What do they want?" Hackerstein asked.

"They didn't say. Yet. Just that if we don't do what they want this plane will explode." It was hard for her to keep her voice steady. She could hear herself going up an octave.

"How much time—?"

"An hour," Cynthia said. She looked at Mr. Hackerstein. He looked almost calm. Maybe he was a bit in shock. She knew she was. The reality of this wasn't sinking in. He moved to go back to his seat and she jumped. No, she wasn't a bit nervous. Not at all.

"Just tap me on the shoulder when you need me," Hackerstein said.

"Sure thing," Cynthia said as she moved slowly down the aisle, trying to look normal. She checked her watch. 3:14. Only 45 minutes left.

The message

"Herb, is that you?" came over the phone from the tower.

"Herb 'Be Right' Stark right here." His joking tone didn't ring true.

"Herb, we've got their demands. They want you to fly the plane to Afghanistan—"

"I knew it!"

" After you dismantle the bomb, that is."

"I knew it was the Afghanis! I don't know we have the fuel for that."

" As a sign of good faith they want us to clear flight path for you and to tell the Afghanis you're coming. And they want amnesty for everyone involved."

"And—?"

"That's it so far. Needless to say, the tower is meeting all of those demands."

"Roger. So how do we go about this?"

"Give Hackerstein a headset."

" Then what?"

"You're to let him into the guts of the plane and they will relay instructions."

"Won't this look a little funny?"

"Well, just tell the passengers that there's been a little trouble with the air conditioning."

"You think they'll buy that?"

"I don't know. Just don't have anyone let out a panic vibe. Keep cool."

"Roger. Cynthia, please get Mr. Hackerstein. And pick up an extra headset on the way."

The instructions

Cynthia put the headset on Hackerstein It gave out a squeal. She adjusted it.

"Now, Mr. Hackerstein, can you hear me?"

"Roger."

" I don't mind telling you that this is a first for all of us. And a good deal is riding on your ability at this point."

"Thank you, Captain. I know. I hope I can do it right."

"They tower will be relaying instructions to you. Cynthia will guide you into the bowels of the plane and they will take it from there. And for all our sakes, don't panic. And don't antagonize them."

"I'll try, Captain."

"Better than try. That's not the kind of language we'd hear in the air force. You'd damn well better succeed."

Henry swallowed. He was not big on dealing with authority and his years in the army had borne that out. "Yes, Sir," he said.

"You OK?" she asked. He nodded.

Outside he kept his eyes straight ahead as she opened the hatch to the avionics bay and he went in.

"Are you reading us, Mr. Hackerstein?" came a voice over the headset.

"Yes, yes," he said.

"A bit louder, please."

"YES!" he bellowed.

"Now we're getting these instructions from the terrorist group. We pass them along just as they say them. If anything is unclear, just ask us to repeat. We don't want any unnecessary mistakes."

"Yes," he said.

"Face the front of the aircraft. On your right you will see shelving with electronic consoles. One console is light blue."

"Yes."

"Right next to this there is a panel, a vertical panel. You should be able to push it open by using the heel of your palm. Push it on the top and the bottom will open. Are you following?"

"I'm looking for the light blue panel." He walked around in the dim light. "I found it." He put pressure on the panel and it grudgingly gave way. "I've got it."

"Now the bomb will be very delicate. Don't be rocking it or slapping it. There should be a green tote bag and the bomb is inside that. Do you see it?"

"I see it!"

"Now pull the bag out gently. Use both hands. Do you have it?"

"What do I do once I get the tote bag out?"

"They haven't said yet. Try to be calm, Mr. Hackerstein. Don't go above deck just yet. Wait for further instructions."

"I'm waiting," he said. "I'm waiting."

****

"Now, Herb, we've got word that Hackerstein has found the bomb. But before they tell us how to dismantle it, they want you to change course and start for Afghanistan. We've done a quick flight plan and we're clearing the way ahead of you. It should be coming over the console about now. Do you see it?"

"Not yet," said Herb.

"Well, give it a minute."

Herb took a deep breath and tried to concentrate on the readings on the dashboard ahead of him. Fuel was OK but not for such a long flight.

"How are they going to know we've changed course?" Herb asked.

"I'm guessing that they're in contact with their man, or woman, on the plane. Do you have any idea of who that might be?"

Herb looked at Cynthia. "Anyone look suspicious to you, kid?" he asked.

Cynthia scrambled her recollection quickly, running over the passenger list in her mind. The Middle Eastern/Islamic names or faces were the obvious choice, but somehow that didn't send up any red flags. She shook her head.

"Well, keep thinking, will ya?" Herb instructed. "Oh! My gosh. What am I thinking? Billy, get one of those cops that are travelling with the prisoner and question him. And on your way back check in the cabin and see if anyone looks suspicious. Let me know immediately."

Cynthia nodded. She looked at her watch: 3:45. Half an hour left.

The cop

"Will you come with me please," Billy Bronze, the co-pilot, said when he reached the two cops.

"Which one?" they both asked at once and laughed. Billy shrugged.

"Toss you, Jerry," said Hank sipping his drink.

"You stay here, I'll go," said Jerry getting out of his seat. He followed the co-pilot to the rear of the plane which was fairly deserted.

"We've gotten a message from the terminal. There was a bomb there which injured eight including custodial staff. It's a group calling themselves 'Hole in One' and they say there's a bomb on board as well."

Jerry let out a low whistle.

"They're asking the air marshal to track the bomb and will give further instructions. I just wanted to know if you think your guy could be involved."

"What do they want?" Jerry asked, shifting from leg to leg.

"They want us to fly to Afghanistan," Bronze said.

Jerry shook his head. "This is all news to me. My guy is being extradited on a multiple murder charge. Nothing political as far as I know."

"Do you think the political thing could just be a hoax to somehow keep your guy from getting to your destination? I mean what is he facing?"

"Probably life in prison, but you know the general public. You can show them a tape of someone being murdered and convince them it's just a movie. No certain outcome as yet."

Bronze took it in. "I'm just as up in the air as you are, no pun here." Both of them chuckled lightly. "We haven't gotten any further instructions yet. As soon as I do, I'll tell Cynthia to let you know. Unless it looks like we could use more help with the passengers. First class is pretty empty?"

Jerry nodded. "Just me, Hank and the man in orange. I think there's a lady passenger, too."

"You keep thinking about a possible tie in. If you can do it without suspicion, ask your prisoner if he has any political friends. Don't do it like that, don't raise any red flags. But just kind of feel him out, if you can."

"It might be a bit tough. He's not a talker."

"Well, neither am I but there's a lot more at stake here than personal style."

"I understand," said Jerry.

"And," Bronze turned and looked at him, "we only have 25 minutes."

Unexpected conspirators?

Meanwhile, Cynthia emerged into the cabin trying not to look nervous, trying to assess the behavior of each of the passengers without being obvious. She smiled, but didn't trust herself to keep smiling.

"Is something wrong?" asked Karen Livingston, seated with her aging mother.

"Don't be stupid, Karen!" snapped Olivia Livingston. "Karen is always imagining some kind of problem where there isn't one."

"You're the one who thought I left the package in the terminal," Karen retorted.

"Did you see a package in the terminal?" Cynthia was immediately on guard.

"I certainly did!" Olivia said. "She brought an extra bag and left it in the terminal."

"That's not so, Mother," Karen protested.

"I'm sorry but I'm going to have to ask you to come with me," Cynthia said firmly.

"I don't understand," Karen began.

"Please stand up and follow me," Cynthia was insistent. She put her hand on Karen's forearm and pulled her up gently. "Don't make a fuss."

Karen went more easily than Cynthia had hoped. They reached the rear of the plane. Cynthia did not relinquish her hold. She motioned to Bronze.

"This young woman was seen leaving a package in the terminal."

"Is that so?" Bronze snapped to attention. "What was in this package?" he demanded, looking from Cynthia to Karen who was starting to wilt.

"There was no package," she squirmed. "My mother is 92. She is borderline delusional. There was no package."

"I'll take it from here, Cynthia," said Bronze. "You go back and ask the mother what exactly she saw."

Cynthia nodded. She went to question Mrs. Livingston.

"My mother said there was luggage," said Karen. "I didn't leave any luggage. We have two bags checked and two in the overhead. And two totes. She's making this up. Whenever I take a few extra minutes she thinks I'm abandoning her. I only went to the gift shop!"

Bronze stiffened. "What for?" he asked.

"I wanted a magazine. I didn't think it was a big deal."

"What magazine?" he asked, tension mounting.

"Vogue."

"Do you have it with you?"

"I changed my mind. I knew she would disapprove." Karen looked totally miserable. Try as he might, Bronze had a tough time fitting her into the profile of a terrorist.

Cynthia returned. "Sorry, the mother doesn't remember any luggage. She now says that Karen brought a bag of food for the plane and left it in the terminal."

"I brought sandwiches for the flight," said Karen. "You can check in the seat ahead of me; the wrappers should still be there." She began to wring her hands.

"Cynthia, go check," said Bronze.

Karen was fidgeting and looking very nervous. "What is this about?" she asked. And then it hit her. "Is there a bomb on the plane?" The co-pilot was silent. "Oh, my god, there's a bomb!" She collapsed into the corner. The co-pilot jumped up and caught her. He steadied her and gave her a slight shake.

Cynthia returned. "Now Mrs. Livingston doesn't remember anything. I found the sandwich wrappers." She turned to Karen.

"I'm sorry, young lady," said the co-pilot. "But we have a bit of a situation on our hands. There's been a bomb in the terminal—"

"Oh, my god!" Karen looked like she was going to collapse all over again. "Was anyone hurt?"

"Eight including the custodian but no serious injuries." The co-pilot waited. She seemed genuinely upset. Could it be that she had unwittingly been the agent of a terrorist and didn't realize it?

"Now is the time for you to be honest with us. If there is anything you're hiding, now is the time to come forward. Did anyone give you a package to take on this plane? Or ask you to move anything inside the terminal?"

Karen shook her head and keep on shaking it. "Nothing, no one, nothing." She closed her eyes. "Oh, my god! We're going to die!"

"Did anyone look suspicious to you in the terminal?" Bronze persisted.

Karen sniffed and blew her nose with a Kleenex. She tried to remember. "There was a woman with a dog I remember."

Cynthia nodded.

"Go on," said Bronze.

"But she just seemed a bit goofy. And there was this girl with all this Native American silver jewelry I remember; she had trouble going through the airport security because she kept on beeping."

Bronze nodded at Cynthia to remember this.

"And the other passengers who came on with us," Karen recalled, sniffing again.

"Well, if you remember anyone or anything else," the co-pilot said, "don't hesitate. And I would appreciate you keeping this to yourself." He looked at Cynthia. "Do you think you can do that, young lady?"

Karen sniffed and nodded.

"We don't want a panic on our hands; we've got enough trouble." Bronze winked, trying to make light of it.

Karen nodded and Cynthia showed her back to her seat.

"Tell them," whispered Bronze to Cynthia, "that there was a mix up in the terminal with some luggage. Something like that."

Cynthia nodded.

"And keep looking for anyone suspicious. Anyone seriously suspicious," he added.

Cynthia tried to smile in agreement. "I don't want to be racist, but there is someone on board with a Middle Eastern name and appearance. An Ali Ashad."

"Bring him." The co-pilot seemed exasperated. "Why didn't you say so earlier?"

Cynthia was at a loss.

"Although," the co-pilot mused, "'Hole in One' isn't exactly the first name you would expect from a Muslim organization. But these days, who knows."

****

"What was all that about?" Hank asked as Jerry returned to his seat.

Jerry checked the prisoner briefly. He seemed asleep. Jerry winked at Hank as he jostled the prisoner, seemingly by accident.

"Oh, it was nothing. The co-pilot has just been asked to provide a list of possible 'friends' of old Sam here that might be waiting for him at the terminal. Hey, Sam! Do you have any sweetie that might show up in Nassau wanting to throw you a kiss?"

Sam stirred himself slightly. "Fat chance," he said.

"I don't know but when I was your age," Jerry continued, "there were a lot of cute co-eds that I couldn't wait to get to know better. Especially, and you're going to laugh at this, I used to go to political rallies just to meet chicks."

"You're putting me on," Hank said, motioning the stewardess for another drink. Jerry put his hand out to stop him, sniffing slightly and Hank began to catch on.

"Tell me more," Hank said.

"Well, I'm sure you had a similar experience, Hank," Jerry said. "What about you, Sam? Don't you think those political chicks are really hot and easy?"

Sam shrugged. "No more so than any other chick."

"Oh, I can't believe that. A stud like you. Maybe you just never hooked up with the right group." Jerry was waiting to see if he would bite.

Sam shrugged again. "I have to take a leak," he said.

"I'll go," said Jerry, stepping back into the aisle. "Or maybe you prefer the exotic type. A big blonde California surf type like yourself must have his pick. Ever date a foreign chick?"

Sam was stumbling as the plane shook slightly.

"I never ask them where they're from," Sam said. Jerry shuddered inwardly. Sam was being held on eight counts of murder, all women. He allegedly picked them up on his motorcycle, rode them into a deserted spot, raped and tortured them and then killed them. He was reported to be pretty much of a loner, so Jerry didn't think that the political angle really applied. But you could never tell. Maybe one crazy chick was following him in the papers and decided to concoct a phony organization to shake things up and spring him loose. Look at Charlie Manson and his "family." Jerry had learned that there were no hard and fast rules when it comes to psychos.

Jerry waited outside the restroom door and listened to hear anything suspicious. The plane took another bump. He hoped that the bomb was not a sensitive one. He checked his watch. Twenty minutes to go.

****

"Mr. Ashad, please come with me," Cynthia said when she reached his seat.

Ali nodded slightly and stood up, smoothing his attire.   Cynthia walked behind him and to the rear of the plane.

"What is this about? "

"The co-pilot will be along in a minute," said Cynthia.

He paused and took in her serious demeanor. The co-pilot was right behind her.

Bronze gave Ashad a long look. Yes, he was a Middle Easterner with the turban and the tunic, the dark complexion and the beard. Somehow he seemed a little too composed. If he were working with the terrorists surely by now he would betray some sense of victory? A smile? A smirk of superiority?

"Do you have any contacts in the Bahamas, Mr. Ashad?" the co-pilot asked.

"I have friends," Ali said.

"What is the purpose of your visit?"

"I have answered all these questions for airport security," Ali said.

"Yes, and now we are asking them again," the co-pilot was brusque.

"I am joining friends and together we are starting a Muslim school for the young children in our community."

"And why, may I ask, are you flying all the way across the country to join this school?"

"Surely this is a free country," Ali had to watch himself. He was on the verge of being sarcastic and perhaps this was not the right time. "I have a degree in early childhood education from New York University," he admitted, more to the point.

The co-pilot sighed. This was not looking like a bomber to him. Not even a very sophisticated bomber. "What is your specialty, if I may ask?"

"I have been trained in autism and speech therapy. Many members of our community have faced persecution," he looked at the captain with eyes ablaze, "and the resulting insecurities have been transmitted to the children. There is a higher incidence of stuttering among the Muslim population, both in New York and in other cities in America."

Now Billy Bronze definitely felt embarrassed. "I'm sorry, Mr. Ashad, but we are facing some—" he fumbled for a word, "difficulties at the terminal and we were asked to inquire further of some of the passengers."

Ali nodded. He was about to ask why none of the other passengers were called away, when he remembered that others had been accompanying the stewardess earlier. He decided better of it.

"Thank you, Mr. Ashad, for your cooperation," said Bronze.

Ali gave a slight bow and went back to his seat.

Jake Talenkov, aka Red Sky

"Stewardess, I'd like another drink, if you please," Jake Talenkov waved his hand as Cynthia passed.

"Just a moment, the steward will be glad to help you," she said, motioning for Happy to give her a hand.

"I'd rather you," Jake reached up and put his hand on her forearm. She yanked her arm away.

"Hey! That's no way to act, honey!" Jake was getting a little bit tipsy.

Cynthia tried to smile. "Hap!" she called out, hoping he would turn around. The passenger's hand was again on her forearm and again she yanked it away, this time more forcefully. To both of their surprise, a thin knife slipped out of his coat sleeve and clambered to the floor. She was quick enough to retrieve it, and step back from the passenger just as Happy approached.

"Hap, I think you'd better escort Mr.—? to the rear of the plane," Cynthia was shaking. She held the knife towards his throat but far enough away that he could not lunge at her. "Get the cop from first class to help you."

Hap was back in a flash with Jerry who was pulling out a spare set of handcuffs.

"What is this? Just because I wanted a little drink?" Talenkov protested. Cynthia handed Jerry the knife.

"This fell out of his sleeve," she said.

"I wonder how that got past the metal detectors," Jerry smiled. "Plastic?"

"That's not mine! This is a frame up!" Talenkov objected. He looked around him at the passengers who were alternately cringing and fascinated.

"Save it, Mister," Jerry yanked Talenkov from his seat and pushed him roughly down the aisle.

Once in the rear of the plane, Jerry pushed Talenkov into the extra jump seat.

"Mr.Bronze, I think we've found the man you're looking for," Jerry smiled.

Bronze looked from Jerry to Talenkov who was squirming in the cuffs. "Good work. How did you identify him?"

"He more or less identified himself," Jerry said, showing Bronze the thin knife. "It fell out of his sleeve when he was trying to paw the flight attendant."

"That's a lie. That's a downright lie! I don't paw anyone. She was coming on to me. The knife is hers! You know there's no way I could get on the plane with a knife like that!"

Bronze looked at Jerry. "Well," the co-pilot said, "we'll have to leave that to Homeland Security to sort out." He got on the phone to the tower. "We've got the terrorist here; we caught him with a knife." The co-pilot turned to Talenkov. "How does it feel to be trapped, Mr. Hole in One?"

Talenkov looked from the co-pilot to Jerry. "What is this 'Mr. Hole in One'? I am Jake Talenkov! From Brooklyn." He gulped rather sharply.

"Yeah, and I'm Willy Mays," said Bronze. "What?" he listened to his head set. "Okay, Mr. Hole in One, tell us how to dismantle the bomb or we're all done for."

"I am not this 'Mr. Hole in One'. I know nothing about a bomb! What bomb?" Talenkov now was beginning to be extremely nervous. Sweat started trickling down his neck. "Someone is pulling some kind of trick on you. I don't know nothing about a bomb." Talenkov tried not to remember the dozen or so times he had used a simple remote control bomb as a diversion. It was important that he convince them of his innocence.

"Don't pretend you're innocent," Bronze demanded. "We have less than five minutes left. The bomb is set to go off. Cynthia! Have you heard anything from Mr. Hackerstein?"

Cynthia shook her head no.

"Get him on the headset. Here, put this Hole in One on with him." She did as she was told. "Now you're going to tell this man on the other end how to dismantle this bomb and stop it from exploding. Or you will die along with everyone else. There'll be no trip to Afghanistan or anywhere else."

Talenkov laughed despite himself. "I don't know who you think I am but I have no intention of going to Afghanistan. Whoever told you this nonsense is really making a big joke of you."

"This is no joke!" Bronze exclaimed. "Don't you try any more of your funny stuff! We've got you and now you're going to—"

And at that moment all the lights in the plane went off leaving them all in the dark.

Technical difficulties

"What's happening?" someone yelled. They could hear a commotion coming from the passengers.

"What the hell—?"another voice interjected.

"Jerry, don't let Talenkov out of those handcuffs!" someone yelled.

"I've got him! Don't worry!"

"You idiots!" Talenkov?

"You'd better come clean, Talenkov! This is no time for fun and games." Bronze commanded. Even though it was already 4 PM and visibility was less than perfect. "How you think we're going to fly you to your Afghanistan is beyond me. We can't do this without electrical support. Is the computer operational?" He reached around and grabbed the arm of someone behind him.

"Cynthia?"

"Yes."

"Hackerstein's not answering on the headset. Go and get him. See what he can come up with. Go!"

****

Cynthia moved slowly up the aisle. She could see dimly. Passengers were getting up from their seats, straining at the windows.

"What's happening?" asked an older woman.

Cynthia tried to be reassuring. "It's just a temporary problem with the electricity; we'll have it back in a few moments."

She got to the hatch leading to the avionics bay and opened it. "Mr. Hackerstein? Mr. Hackerstein?" she called out. There were no lights inside the plane either.

"Coming out," Hackerstein said. She could see the sweat on his neck and shirt collar.

"What's happening?" she asked in a whisper. "We don't have any electricity."

"I must have made a mistake," he said sheepishly.

"A mistake." Cynthia couldn't keep the anguish out of her voice. "We're facing a bomb and you make a mistake. Didn't you follow the instructions?"

"I thought I did," Hackerstein shrugged.

"Just remain calm," Cynthia said. "The co-pilot wants to see you."

Hackerstein nodded.

Billy Bronze moved up to the front of the plane. He had brought Talenkov and Jerry up to first class with him.

Cynthia introduced them in the dark. "Mr.Bronze, Mr. Hackerstein."

"I made a mistake," Hackerstein shrugged.

"What the—!" Bronze was furious. "Didn't you have the headset? Weren't they talking to you? What happened? What went wrong?"

"What headset?" Talenkov asked Jerry. "What the hell is going on here?"

"You shut up!" Jerry glared at Talenkov.

"Did you dismantle the bomb or not?" the co-pilot demanded of Hackerstein.

Hackerstein shrugged. "I don't know."

"You don't know! What kind of answer is that? You don't know!"

"I mean I did everything that they told me to do."

"And—?"

"And the lights went off," Hackerstein admitted. "Maybe that means the bomb is dismantled. Maybe the electrical shut down also dismantled the bomb?'"

Bronze took in Hackerstein's suggestion.

"Beats me," Bronze admitted. He turned to Hackerstein. "What exactly did they tell you to do?"

"I, I don't remember exactly," Hackerstein began.

"Well, tell us what you do remember," Bronze prompted.

"They told me to find the light blue panel and then there was this other panel next to it," Hackerstein began.

"Yes," Bronze was impatient.

"There were all these complicated things I was supposed to do, " Hackerstein continued. He shrugged again.

"Yes," Bronze said.

"I must confess," Hackerstein said, "I don't totally remember them all."

"He doesn't remember them all," Bronze was fuming.

"Billy, what's the difference?" Cynthia cut in. "The bomb didn't go off.   It's already past four PM and the bomb didn't go off."

They all sighed a sigh of relief. There was some applause and a bit of nervous laughter.

"And we caught the terrorist." Bronze continued. "So it's alright."

"I am not a terrorist," Talenkov protested loudly. "I do not engage in such childish nonsense."

"Shut up!" Jerry prodded him.

"No, you shut up, Mr. Big City Cop Who Doesn't Know His Ass From His Elbow! I am not a terrorist! I am not the person you're looking for! Don't you think if I were I would have stopped the bomb? What makes you think there ever was a bomb to begin with?"

There was a silence.

"There was a bomb in the terminal. Eight people were injured," Cynthia volunteered.

"So?" Talenkov continued. "So? It's easy to plant one bomb and say there's another. What proof do you have that there was another bomb? This man," he pointed to Hackestein, "doesn't even know what he did that made the electricity go off! What makes you think he stopped the bomb? What makes you think there even was a bomb?"

There was another uneasy silence.

"There was a bomb," Hackerstein said. "I heard it ticking." He paused. "And then I didn't hear it ticking."

"You see?" Cynthia said. "There was a bomb! This man,"she pointed to Talenkov, "is just trying to confuse things."

"No! You are the one who is confused!" Talenkov continued. "'I heard ticking'! Well maybe it was the ticking of his own watch, or the sound of his own coward's heart he heard!"

"I am not a coward!" Hackerstein fumed. "I am more brave than you will ever know!"

"Oh? Is that so, Mr. Turn Off the Electricity And Jam Up the Plane?" Talenkov laughed.

"So where does that leave us now?" Jerry asked. He looked at Talenkov. Somehow the man looked strangely familiar.

"What are your demands now?" Bronze asked Talenkov. "I don't know you're in much of a position to demand anything."

"He isn't, but I am."

Everyone turned around at a new person entering the discussion.

The terrorist

It was difficult   to make out her form at first.

"Mrs. Krutz!" Cynthia gasped.

The tall woman in her 50's smiled. "You can call me 'Hole in One'."

A suppressed gasp ran through the assembly.

"Oh, you're all so smart. You thought the big bad terrorist had to be a man." She laughed. She turned to Hackerstein. "It's alright, Henry, I'll take it from here." Hackerstein stepped forward and handed Mrs. Krutz the small tote bag he take taken from inside the plane. She took a revolver from the bag.

"You two—?" Jerry asked in amazement.

"Yes, we two," Mrs. Krutz said smugly.

"You said you'd keep me out of this!" Hackerstein protested.

"A little late for that now, Henry," Mrs. Krutz shrugged.

"How the hell—?" Bronze asked.

"Simple," Mrs. Krutz was proud of her work. "I instructed Henry how to get into the computer system on the plane and now I control the whole shooting match, in manner of speaking." She raised the revolver and the metal gleamed. "Not all computer whizzes are teen aged guys with thick glasses and bad social skills."

"What do you hope to get from this?" Stark was intent.

"You'll find out soon enough," Mrs. Krutz said. "Henry, you can go back and watch the cabin. Remember, report everything to me immediately."

Henry nodded.

"You see, I told you I had nothing to do with it," Talenkov said. "Now you can remove these silly things from my wrists."

Jerry looked at the co-pilot.

"Why are you looking at him?" Mrs. Krutz asked. "I'm the one with the gun, and the bomb, and the only one who really knows what's going on here."

"I wouldn't be so sure of that," Billy Bronze interjected.

"Shut up!" Mrs. Krutz snapped. "You just sit tight, nobody make any sudden movements and do what I tell you and everything will work out as planned."

The new commander

"First thing I want to assure you that I am 100% serious. In case you had any doubts. I have here," Mrs. Krutz indicated the tote bag that Hackerstein had passed to her, "a very efficient and unassuming little bomb that can and will be set in motion if I have any suspicion that you are trying what they call in the movies any 'funny stuff'." She smiled and patted her chest with the hand holding the gun.

"You do realize that you will be blown sky high, so to speak, along with the rest of us," Bronze couldn't refrain from reminding her.

"Oh, yes, I know that. But like all true revolutionaries I have nothing to lose and quite a good deal to gain," Mrs. Krutz kept nodding her head.

"And what are we gaining by going to Afghanistan?" Jerry asked.

"Glad you asked, Mr. Handcuffs Up The Ass Policeman. We're not going to Afghanistan. We're going on a little detour."

"But the instrument panel isn't working," Bill Bronze protested. "How are we even going to be able to land or even correct the course?" Everyone was looking around at everyone else. This was the first time it had occurred to many of them that without controls, radar or contact with the ground they were going to have a tough time getting anywhere in the plane. Especially now that night would be falling, it would be difficult to find a place for a safe landing.

"I have taken care of that," Mrs. Krutz beamed. "First all of you get over here. Policeman, I want you to cuff yourself and co-pilot together. And I want all of you to stand in this side of the plane. Where I can keep an eye on you. Little Miss Stewardess, I want you to sit here while I take the controls."

"But I don't know what to do," Cynthia protested.

"You don't have to know. You just have to know how to keep your mouth shut and do what I tell you. Do you think you can do that?"

Cynthia nodded. She swallowed hard. Her mouth was dry with fear.

Mrs. Krutz took a seat and opened up a small tablet. The light illuminated her face. "Watch and you may learn something," she beamed. "I have connected my computer to avionics on this plane."

"She had the air marshal make the connection," Bill Bronze whispered.

"A plus for the co-pilot. You're not as dumb as you might appear. And do you want to tell everyone what I can accomplish? Well?"

"It enables you to take over the controls and fly the plane," Bronze said softly.

"A bit louder; I don't think everyone heard you," Mrs. Krutz commanded.

"It enables you to take over all the controls and fly the plane," Bronze said more loudly.

"Correct! So you don't really have to know anything at this point except that if any of you try and stop me there will be dire consequences. I may even get so nervous that I lose control completely and we go into a nose dive. After all, what am I but a simple unskilled woman with more than a screw loose? Hey?" Mrs. Krutz laughed.

Everyone exchanged glances. The light in the sky was fading more and more rapidly.

"Come on, Mr. Hackerstein!" Mrs. Krutz yelled. "Join the party."

"I got the cop to cuff himself to his seat and I got his gun," Hackerstein was waving it back and forth.

"Take it easy, Hackerstein!" Mrs. Krutz cautioned. "You don't want to be close enough to any of these yokels so that they can grab the gun away from you. Now hand me the policeman's gun and take out your own gun."

Hackerstein's did as instructed.

" If anything should go wrong," Mrs. Krutz continued, "I could just take this gun and shoot a hole or holes through the plane and get us started on a downward spiral. Just remember that."

"But what are you trying to accomplish?" Bronze baited her. "What the hell is the purpose of all of this? We don't have any special cargo. Do you want his prisoner?" He indicated the cop and Sam Blank.

"Watching too much TV, are we?" Mrs. Krutz smirked at her little joke. "No, this is a lot more serious. Ladies and gents, you are going to be part of the first and perhaps the last Electronic Take Over of the United States of America, engineered and accomplished with the minimum of man or woman power and a maximum of effectiveness. And do you know how I'm going to do that? Mr. Co-Pilot? You were so on the money before; do you want to take a guess?"

"No, I'm out of ideas," Bronze said roughly.

"Well, listen closely, boys and girls. You might just learn something. Just a moment, I have to adjust the course." And Mrs. Krutz typed in some information on her computer and began pushing buttons on the console.

"I sure hope she knows what she's doing," Bronze said.

"That makes two of us," Cynthia replied while the rest waited in intense silence.

Change of flight plans

The silence at the front of the plane was only punctuated by the soft click of Mrs. Krutz's fingers on her keyboard. There was a slight glow from the electricity on her small instrument and still a bit of twilight coming through the windows.

Every one of those present could hear their own breathing and their own heartbeats.

"Aha!" Mrs. Krutz announced dramatically as she pushed the final key on the keyboard. "Just wait and see!"

They did not have long to wait. As Mrs. Krutz took control of the plane, they began a rapid descent, an accelerating nose dive. Everyone froze. There was a sharp intake of breath. Then just as suddenly there was a jolt as they began to level off.   Mrs. Krutz started to turn the plane around. They were heading back in the opposite direction.

"What the hell—?" Bronze exclaimed. "What is going on here?"

"Don't you wish you knew?" Mrs. Krutz chuckled. "Don't you wish you knew?" She paused dramatically. "We're headed for a different landing, a new target, if you will. Very soon, very soon." She smiled and began to hum to herself.

Bronze tried to see out the window, but only saw dim lights of a city they guessed might be Miami.

"Did you set up the drop?" Mrs. Krutz asked Hackerstein.

Hackerstein nodded. "Just like you said,"

"Excellent! Then we don't have long to wait."

"What drop?"Bronze asked.

"Well, since you want to know, when Mr. Hackerstein was so kind to fiddle with the innards of this plane, I also had him set up another small bomb that will be released in about—" here she checked her watch, "about ten minutes! Bombs away!" And she began laughing manically.

"But what's the target? What's the purpose?" Cynthia asked with a mixture of outrage and confusion.

Bronze shrugged. "Don't' know. And I don't know if you want to ask her," he indicated Mrs. Krutz.

"I hear your little whispers," Mrs. Krutz said. "Control! That is the purpose! Control of it all! How about the government? Does the Bay of Pigs ring a bell with any of you hot shots? Or are you too young to remember?"

"Cuba," Bronze whispered hoarsely.

"That's why there are no escorting planes," Cynthia said.

"Go to the head of the class," Mrs. Krutz smiled. "Who would be stupid enough to risk an international incident when only one plane of a measly 100 people is at stake?"

"I can't believe she would actually do this," Cynthia said. "Why? Didn't they go along with your demands?"

Mrs. Krutz shrugged.

"But what happens if you release a bomb over Cuba? Won't there be a incident then?" Bronze asked.

"Well' just have to see, won't we," Mrs. Krutz's voice was rich with self-satisfaction. "We'll just have to see." Mrs. Krutz turned around. "Mr. Hackerstein and stewardess, please return to the main cabin and keep the passengers calm. And remember if you try anything it will be the last move you will ever make."

The reasons?

"So what is the purpose off all this? What was the 'Hole in One' business about?" Bronze asked.

"She's a fake!" came the low voice from a dark corner. It was Talenkov. "She's no terrorist. There is no agenda. She's an anarchist and a poor excuse for one at that."

"Watch your mouth, Mister!" Mrs. Krutz turned the plane sharply to one side so everyone was forced to hold on to the wall in order to remain upright.

"She just wants money," Talenkov continued.

Mrs. Krutz let out a prolonged laugh. "Oh, you simple soul. If money was all I wanted I would have used my skills to rob the banks. I would have set up accounts and diddled the computers of all the stock markets and the brokers and the big corporations. International accounts. Money is not everything. Money! One dollar bill is just like another, but an hour lost will never come again."

"Who said that? Benjamin Franklin?" said Bronze.

"No, Mr. Co-pilot. I said that," said Mrs. Krutz. "And for whatever portion of your life remains you will be able to ponder its wisdom."

Another round

Hackerstein and Cynthia returned to the main cabin.

"Why are the lights out?" young Jesse Lovehill asked.

"The computer system is having problems, honey," Cynthia said as she offered him a bag of peanuts.

"Maybe I can help," Jesse volunteered.

"That's very sweet of you, honey. Maybe later," Cynthia turned to Hackerstein and pushed the drink cart towards him. "Here, you steer," she said as the handle of the cart hit his stomach.

"I'd like a scotch," said Ethiopia Beldez.

"Certainly," said Cynthia. "And because of the inconvenience, Madam, the drinks are courtesy of the airline."

A general murmur of approval went out along with exclamations of "Champagne anyone?" and "Make mine a double," and "That's more like it!"

Cynthia glanced at Hackerstein who was trying to pass a small bottle of booze and a cup to Ethiopia Beldez without falling over.

"Why is it dark outside?" Holly Nash asked the stewardess.

"Nighttime, " Cynthia replied quickly as she gave her a gin and tonic.

"Oh, and I thought I would be able to buy the young lady a drink," James Cologne smiled. He lifted his glass in Holly's direction and tipped his head.

"Thanks, " said Holly as the stewardess handed her a drink.

"Do you mind me joining you?" James asked as he moved up the aisle to where Holly was seated.

Holly shrugged and moved over.

"Honey, I hope you don't take this the wrong way," said James as he took off his sunglasses, "but haven't I met you somewhere before?"

Holly shook her head.

"I thought maybe we might have known some of the same people. One of my friends in Philadelphia had a girlfriend who looked a lot like you."

"Never been to Philadelphia," Holly said sipping her drink.

"I could be wrong," James said. "I remember thinking, 'Man, this chick is hot!' I hope that doesn't offend you?" He watched her reaction.

She smiled. "And now that I'm not the same chick what do you think?"

"I still think 'Man, this chick is hot!' but now I don't have to worry that I'm getting into a brother's territory, you know?"

Holly pushed her hair over her shoulder and took another sip. "And what do you do for a living?"

"I'm in computers. It's a growing industry. One that's just getting off the ground, if you'll excuse the pun."

Holly just kept on drinking.

"What about you?"

"Well, it's funny you should ask, because I just took a class in computers myself."

"That so. How'd ya do?"

"I even surprised myself."

"That so. Well, some guys don't like a chick with brains but I think it just makes the chase a little more interesting, don't you think?"

"Bring it on," said Holly.

"Whoah. Hey, stewardess, a couple of more drinks back here. You don't mind, do you, honey?"

"Why quit when you're ahead? Besides, it's not like either of us has to drive."

"You got that right," said James. "So what brings you to the Bahamas? Fun in the sun? Running from someone? I can't believe a fox like you would make a trip like this alone."

"Well, let's just say the last guy I hooked up with is in for a bit of a surprise."

"So he didn't catch you and throw you back?"

"Catch and release? No way. More like he hooked up with a bigger fish than he could handle." She smiled and sipped.

"I like the sound of that. And what if I end up catching you? Would you run away again?"

"No guarantees, mister."

"You know there are laws against breaking someone's heart," James said.

"There you're wrong. Just on how big a price you can charge for it."

"Now this is getting interesting. How much did the last guy pay?"

"He hasn't found out yet."

"And when he does? Any chance of him coming after you?"

"Not if he knows what's good for him. Why, you want to fight for me?"

"I'm already fighting. How am I doing?"

More new friends

"While you're at it, can I have a refill?" Helmut Hardcastle waved his champagne glass in the air. Cynthia was a seat ahead of him to the left, taking care of Nancy Wardhope, aka Goddess of the Mandrake Wold, her mother and Aunt Ethel.

"That sounds good," Nancy turned and looked at Helmut. "I think I'll have champagne too."

"Nancy!" her mother exclaimed.

"Well, it's free, isn't it? And why shouldn't I have a glass? Is it any worse than that gin and tonic you're drinking?" Nancy looked at Helmut and smiled. He winked at her, out of habit.

"Don't I know you?" Aunt Ethel chimed in as she was reaching for her white wine.

Helmut just kept smiling.

"I mean your face is so familiar! Are you on television or in the movies? I know, Channel 474, 'Shop 'til You Drop'! You're Helmut!" Aunt Ethel giggled.

"Guilty as charged," Helmut was pleased to say. Especially now, after being given the axe, it was refreshing to know that there was nothing the studio could do to discourage his fans from finding him irresistible.

"Are you on your way to a special sales conference?" Aunt Ethel asked. She turned to Lucy. "Lucy, this man is the absolute tops! He could sell snow to the Eskimos! Many a time, young man," she smiled at Helmut, "I've taken your fashion advice. Especially about Willy's Wardrobe; there is this line of clothes, Willy's Wardrobe," she confided in Lucy, "that seem to be so simple and almost drab, but when you put them on in the right color and with the right accessories, I mean you look like a million bucks. Style with a smile he calls it. Isn't that so?" She smiled conspiratorially at Helmut.

"When you're right you're right," he nodded. "You seem to have taken my advice to heart," he continued, if I may be so bold." He indicated her lime green long sweater vest over a grey turtleneck and black pants.

"Why, right you are! I didn't even notice! I am so distressed over what is happening on this flight that my priorities went right out of my head." Aunt Ethel was tickled at having recognized a genuine celebrity. "Nancy, you would do well to take some advice from this wonderful gentleman," she continued. "You can see, Helmut, how she wears this dreadful purple nail polish and black lipstick?"

"Aunt Ethel! Helmut," Nancy turned. "My aunt thinks that anyone who is the slightest bit different is asking to join a terrorist organization."

Helmut laughed.

"Certainly," Nancy continued, "individual expression is the cornerstone of a real personal style."

He nodded. "Couldn't agree more."

"My aunt also thinks," Nancy continued, "that by being a witch I am just opening the floodgates for terrorism. What do you think?" She paused dramatically.

Helmut got out of his seat and moved closer to Nancy and her party.

"If you will share the next set of drinks with me," he said with Great Personal Charm, "I promise to tell you what I think about fashion, personal expression and Wicca."

"You know about Wicca?" Nancy was pleasantly surprised.

"I'm English, am I not?" he winked again. "Stonehenge, Pentangle and all that. Stewardess, please give us another round over here! Now what exactly is your area of interest?"

"Well," said Nancy, "I do a little palmistry."

"Is that so? Well, what can you tell me by looking at my palm?"

"Alright. Now give me your left hand. This is what you were born with. Hmmmm. Good strong intellect. You have an unusual way of looking at the world and energy to do things many people wouldn't."

"Now, you're getting a little personal here."

"Should I stop?"

"I'm joking. You're right on the money. And you've piqued my interest. No fair stopping now."

"Well, you have a lot of energy, but I also see a lot of disappointments. Let me see your right hand. This is what you make of your life. At least so far."

"This should be good."

"Yes, I see you've been very fortunate. You have overcome many obstacles. If I had a magnifier I could read your fingerprints."

"Is that significant?"

"Well, they did a study, after fingerprints were discovered and used in identifying criminals. There are three types of fingerprints: the most common which almost everyone has, the whorl which is found among many artists and some creative types and the arch which is found mostly among serious criminals."

"Is that so?"

"The interesting thing is artists and criminals share the whorls."

"Really. Where did you hear that?"

"They did a study. And I've read the palms of people in both categories."

"Don't you think that starving artists become criminals?"

"You're teasing again. But really it's true. I think it's because they both have unusual ways of looking at the world. Do you know the Chinese can read your whole life from the thumb? The thumb has more nerves than anywhere."

"Do go on."

"Oh—"

"What's wrong?"

"Well, it looks like you're going to have a serious accident when you are about 45."

"How serious?"

"Well—"

"Come on, how serious?"

"You might die. But then maybe I'm reading it wrong. How old are you now?"

"46."

The novelist

"Could I please have a white wine? "Enid Snark asked Mr. Hackerstein.

Henry was moving right along dispensing drinks, glad that he didn't have to make change.

"Certainly," he smiled.

"And could you please tell me why exactly you are doing this instead of the regular cabin crew?" Enid lifted her glass to toast him.

Henry started to fumble around for an answer.

"I hope I'm not being too forward," she continued, "but I couldn't help but notice that one by one several of the passengers were called to the rear of the plane. And the lights have gone off. Is there some kind of emergency?"

Henry was silent. He tried to smile. "Computer trouble?" he ventured.

"But why did they ask you to help out?" Enid persisted.

"Well, the other steward knows more about the computer stuff so they asked me to lend a hand."

"And you are—? Oh, please excuse my inquisitiveness. I am a romance novelist and I guess I tend to see the suspense and plot device in any situation."

Henry almost sighed a visible sigh of relief. "Well, that is understandable. And it is a lovely and interesting hobby, to be sure."

"It's not a hobby. I am Enid Snark, author of <u>The Roses Touched Her Fate</u>, the series with names of flowers in the titles." She waited for a reaction. "Surely you have heard of them?"

Hackerstein shook his head. "Oh, wait! My wife is a fan of yours!" He suddenly remembered and was grateful to Henriette for bothering him with her incessant harping on the love affairs of this or that lovely lady in the "flower" books. "She especially likes the gardener—"

"Melissa Small?" Enid was happy to be recognized. "Yes?"

"She says that she feels that this Melissa is a kindred spirit and wishes that she could be born again in the 1800's."

"Why that's the loveliest thing anyone has said to me in a long time!" Enid exclaimed. She sipped more of her wine and the troubles of the plane and any inconsistencies she might have noticed flew right out of her head.

More questions

"Would you like a drink, courtesy of the management?" Cynthia asked the elderly couple.

"I don't know," the wife began, glancing at her husband.

"That sounds like it might be just the thing," he said. "Do you have ouzo?"

"That's a question I've not been asked before," Cynthia said. "That's Greek, isn't it?"

"That's the best, that's what it is," Mr. Solaris said proudly.

"I don't think so. Maybe a brandy?" Cynthia smiled.

"What do you say, Mira?"

"Somehow it seems wrong to celebrate," she said quietly. Cynthia could see that she had been crying.

"We are going to bury our daughter," said Mr. Solaris with some difficulty, putting a brave face on the event.

Cynthia didn't know what to say.

"It's not a celebration of her death, but of her life," Mr. Solaris said firmly. "Here, Mira, don't make this nice young lady sadder than she needs to be."

"Why the free booze?" asked the young man one seat back.

"Our way of apologizing for the lights going out and the delay," said Cynthia.

"What delay? I didn't hear anything about a delay," Mr. Solaris said sharply.

Cynthia hadn't intended to say so much. "Well, it's computer problems and we have to have some time to put things right."

"Are you sure about that? I don't ever recall being on a flight where there were no lights in the cabin," Joseph continued.

"I'm worried, Joseph," said Mira Solaris. "What if—"

"Now, now," said her husband. Maybe he'd better not upset his wife further. "What could happen? They have a little trouble with the electronics and we get there a little later. It's not like Diana will notice." He was silent as the reality of the funeral came back to him.

"I don't know," James Cologne leaned over his seat and entered the conversation. "It's got to be something more. The lights just don't go out like that. And all the music and the movie."

"Well, aren't they all related?" Solaris asked.

"It's not like they're all on one program," James Cologne was showing off. "I mean, if you were to say that all the lights were connected, and the reason we're not seeing any lights on the ground is because somehow it's all related to the computer on the plane, well, then you would be very wrong."

"I didn't notice that," said Mira Solaris. She looked out the window. "Joseph, look! All the lights below on the ground are out!"

"Don't be silly, Mira. There are no lights there. We're flying over water."

"Hey! You're right," said Cologne. He hadn't thought of that. "All the lights are out. We're going over water."

"That's impossible!" said Solaris. "Can't they fix the computers?"

"I don't know," said Cologne. He looked at Holly. "Something really fishy is going on here."

****

"Hey! How about some drinks back here?" Buster called out. He and Joline had a little nap after their initiation into the "mile high" club and now he was ready for another shot.

"Why are they all talking up there?" Joline asked.

"What do you mean, honey?"

"That young guy and that old couple. And the old guy with the stewardess. He wasn't there before."

"Maybe he's a stewardess in training," Buster laughed. "Or maybe-" he pinched Joline, "he's just a horny old guy looking for some action."

"Oh, Buster!" she shrieked.

"Whatever he is, I hope they get here soon or I'm going to go out and bring them back."

"You wouldn't!"

"Wouldn't I? Just you watch me, honey. I am seriously in need of some scotch whiskey and whatever Buster wants—" he looked at her with his head cocked indicating she should finish the sentence.

"Buster gets!" Joline giggled.

"You got that right!" He gave her playful slap on the rump as he eased himself out of his seat. "Hey! You up there with the free booze! How about spreading some of that joy around here?"

Others next to them started a raucous chant. "More booze! More booze! We second that!" Buster smiled, very pleased with himself. He sure knew how to work a crowd. And he didn't even have to pay for this round to be a big shot.

Then he dimly remembered that he did not want to attract attention. Remember those empty deposit boxes with their owners gasping in horror.

"But these guys can't say anything about me, just a guy getting a little happy on his honeymoon. Hey, it would look suspicious if I didn't get a little carried away," he reasoned to himself.

Cynthia Billings and Hackerstein were working the drink cart slowly back to Buster's area. Hackerstein was less practiced than Cynthia in pulling his arm away from the grasp of the thirsty and needy passengers.

"What's happening?" asked Mr. Lovehill. He too had noticed the lack of lights on the ground. "Is the plane in trouble?"

"No, no," said Hackerstein unconvincingly. "Just some computer problems."

"I can fix that!" piped up young Jesse.

"Now that's very nice of you to want to help the pilot," Mrs. Lovehill said. "Isn't that sweet?" she turned to her husband.

Bill Lovehill half ignored his wife. "Where are we now? What city are we near?" he pestered Hackerstein. "Is this going to delay our flight?"

"I'm really not sure," Hackerstein tried to be non-commital and still smile. "Would you like a glass of wine?"

"White please," said Mrs. Lovehill. "And juice for the children."

"I want a ginger ale," said Jonquil. "And I am not a child."

"Very well, ginger ale for the young lady and apple juice for the pilot's helper," Mrs. Lovehill said.

"Why are there no lights on the ground?" Bill Lovehill insisted. "And why are we flying into the darkness, not into the twilight?"

"I'm sure it's just a momentary course correction," Hackerstein said with embarrassment.

"Hey, what about our drinks?" Buster Walker was striding down the aisle just in time to hear Bill Lovehill's last question. He took a quick look out the window.

"And there are no lights on the ground," Lovehill reiterated.

"That's really strange," Buster agreed. "Hey, wait! I see some light there!" He pointed out the nearest window.

"Probably a reflection from a mirror on a car or a house. Or maybe light from a body of water," Lovelhill guessed.

"Would you like your scotch on the rocks?" Cynthia hoped that remembering his drink would flatter him and distract him. Other passengers were beginning to look out the windows as well.

"Yeah, sure," Buster was sobering up. "And white wine for the Mrs."

"Why are there no lights, Daddy?" Jesse Lovehill asked. "Is the computer broken?"

"The lights on the ground aren't connected to the lights on the plane," Lovehill explained, almost embarrassed by his son.

"Aren't they?" Frank James asked. "I mean they both went off at almost the same time."

Buster Walker turned around. "Did they?"

"Yeah, don't you remember? The lights in the plane went out and then in five minutes or less, wham! We turned around and the lights on the ground disappeared."

"That's impossible!" Buster exclaimed. "just a coincidence."

"I don't' know," Frank James said. "I've been watching the Weather Channel's series on plane disasters. And often the loss of controls leads to trouble on the ground. And then—" He raised his eyebrows and nodded his head with solemn drama.

"That's not so." Buster was getting seriously upset. "Is it?" he asked Cynthia.

"No, of course not. It's just a coincidence." She looked at Frank James. "You don't want to panic everyone, do you?"

Frank James got the message when he looked at her frightened eyes.

"No, of course not," he said calmly, keeping his eyes focused on Cynthia's. "I got carried away, that's all." He smiled blandly and hoped that this would allay suspicion.

Just then the plane lurched forwards and all those in the aisle had parts of their drinks spilled all over.

"Hey! Watch it!" Buster Walker exclaimed. "Now I need another white wine!"

Undiscovered talents

"What's that you're drawing there? Can I see?"Sunny asked.

Candy trained her pencil flashlight on her sketch book. "It's from a photo. I'm just doing a sketch of it."

"That's really very good."

"Thank you. The couple there, their daughter died and they're going to pick up her body. This is for the memorial."

"That's a nice idea. Do you know them?"

"Not really. Doggo stole their photo and sort of messed it up so I volunteered."

"That's very generous of you."

"The least I could do."

"Looks like you've got a whole book of them. Can I see?"

"Sure. That's the couple—"

"Very good."

"That's the front of the plane."

"Hmmm."

"That's Doggo at the airport."

"I see."

"And Doggo in the cab."

"Hmmm. And Doggo on your arm?"

"You got that right. Doggo the tattoo. I designed it myself"

"Very impressive. Do you do this for a living?"

"I used to. I was a tattoo artist."

"And?"

"I got sick."

"I don't mean to get nosy."

"No, it's okay. I thought I was taking the proper precautions and then someone with HIV moved suddenly and the needle pricked me. Now I have to take medication."

"That's a drag."

"It could be worse."

"How's that?"

"I could be dead already."

"That's no way to talk."

"Maybe not but I have to face facts. The worst thing is that I've fought too hard to avoid being dependent on others. And now I'm dependent on this medication."

"You shouldn't feel that way. I mean, it's not your fault and you're doing the best you can with the choices you have. I wish I could say the same."

"You're just being nice."

"No, I'm not. I'm really not. I've had plenty of times in my life when I had a choice—quit or keep on. And I mean quit something or someone I knew was bad for me. But I didn't listen to myself. I just kept on going. 'I can stop tomorrow,' I told myself. But I never did. What I regret most is the people I've been hooked up with."

"You look like you did all right."

"Maybe moneywise, but otherwise—I mean you are such a nice and worthwhile person."

"Thank you, but you don't really know me."

"That's true, but I can see you're kind, you're considerate. You love animals—"

"That's true."

"And you go out of your way to be helpful. Look at the drawing for the old couple. I've known lots of chicks who looked great from the outside but when it got down to the wire, it was hasta la vista baby."

"Maybe you've had bad luck."

"You make your own luck. You can't blame luck for everything."

"That's true. You have to work and work. Like my drawing. You have to perfect your craft so when inspiration comes along you have the skill to grab it. You can't wait to create and be inspired.

"In the Japanese puppet theatre, the Bunraku, it takes three people to manipulate a puppet. One does the feet, one does the left hand and the main puppeteer does the right hand. These puppets are almost life sized. All the puppeteers wear black in full view of the audience; only the head puppeteer has his face showing.

"First you sweep the floor for five or ten years, then you do the feet for another ten, and then the left hand. Finally you get to manipulate the head. You have to work up to it for years."

"Where did you learn all this stuff?

"When you're sick you have time to read and to think about things."

"Looks like you made good use of your down time."

"I don't know," Candy paused. "To tell you the truth, I've reached a point in my life when I'm faced with a big decision. I thought I had made it; now I'm sort of—"

"Is that so? I feel like I'm facing a big turning point in my life as well." Sonny stopped, sensing her hesitation. "I mean it's not a competition."

"Believe me, you don't want to go where I'm going."

"How can you say that? Surely things can't be that bad. Try me."

"Worse than you can imagine." Candy paused. "I've left the country for good."

"What?" Sonny was stunned. "A wanted woman, eh?"

"I've reached the point where I'm not making enough money for my medical expenses—"

"What about black market drugs?"

"That's not the main point. I'm getting sicker and sicker and I just don't feel it's worth it. You just don't want to get up, take medicine, monitor the medicine, adjust the medicine—everything revolves around the sickness, the constant grind of continuing illness. It becomes your whole life. And seeing the doctor is the high point."

"What makes you think I don't know?" Sonny asked.

Candy took a breath. "I going where assisted suicide is an option."

Sonny didn't know what to say.

"Don't tell anyone," Candy continued. "I don't want to be stopped."

"I can't believe this," Sonny said.

"You don't know what it's like to wake up every day and have no energy except to maintain your vital signs and take medicine. "

"Hey, wait a minute! You don't know anything about me. What if I told you that I'm a serious drug addict and I'm just about to clean up my act, go cold turkey? That I maybe have some people after me?" Sonny stopped. He'd said too much.

"You're just saying that to make me feel better," Candy said, blowing her nose.

Sonny laughed. "Well, if this isn't the most ridiculous conversation. Both of us making things out to be as bad as they can be. Listen," he took her hand. "What if we try to cheer each other up? It can't get any worse, can it?"

"Promise not to try to talk me out of it?" Candy asked.

"Now, I didn't say that, did I? Besides, I'll bet you try to encourage me to get healthy and how hypocritical would that be if I know you're planning on doing away with yourself?"

Candy laughed in spite of herself.

"Besides, who is going to take care of this fellow here?" Sunny patted Doggo. Doggo barked.

Candy sniffed.

"No more tears, not for now," Sonny said and squeezed her hand.

Change and change again

Hackerstein looked at his watch. It was time for him to check back in with Mrs. Krutz. He exchanged glances with Cynthia.

He went to the first class section.

"It's Hackerstein here," said.

Inside the front galley it was darker than he had remembered. Only the glow from Mrs. Krutz's computer lit up the space. He could hear shuffling and coughing.

"Come on! Come on! Join the fun!" Mrs. Krutz's voice boomed out.

"When are we going to refuel?" he asked. There was a long pause.

"Change of plans," Mrs. Krutz said.

"What change?" asked Hackerstein.

"We're not refueling."

"Then how can we get to Afghanistan?"

"Glad you asked. We're not going to Afghanistan. Try to keep up, Henry," Mrs. Krutz said with buoyant finality.

"But—" Hackerstein was dumbfounded. "That was the deal! We were supposed to go to Afghanistan! I was supposed to get out when we refueled! My wife—" he sputtered.

"Sorry, Henry. Wrong script."

"But you can't do that! We had an agreement! They told me—"

"Who is 'they'?" asked Jerry, the cop.

"Shut your mouth!" Mrs. Krutz barked.

"But we had an agreement!" Hackerstein pleaded. "You just can't change it! They won't let you."

"Who is 'they'?" Jerry insisted.

"And who is to stop me?" Mr. Krutz's voice turned nasty. "You can't do anything about it!"

"This can't be happening! I made an agreement with them!" Hackerstein's voice was shrill.

"Who are 'they'?" Jerry persisted.

"The government! The government! The CIA!" Hackerstein yelled. "They will stop you! I swear it!"

"The CIA!" Jerry exclaimed.

"Well, I'll be damned. I think our terrorist is a government agent," Billly Bronze said.

"Well, then, that's wonderful. We can just turn the plane around and stop all this silliness," Jerry was relieved.

"I don't think it's so simple," said Bronze. "I think she's gone rogue."

"What the hell does that mean?"

"Why don't you ask Hackerstein, our air marshal?" Bronze suggested, hoping to set up a confrontation.

"You keep your mouth shut, Hackerstein!" Mrs. Krutz snarled. "If you know what's good for you!"

"We had a deal!" Hackerstein yelled. "You can't just change it! I'll call—" he fumbled for his cell phone.

"That won't work up here, Hackerstein," Mrs. Krutz said. "I've jammed the circuits."

"You can't do that!" Hackerstein kept trying his phone.

"Can and will," Mrs. Krutz's voice was on an even keel once more.

"So why would the CIA want to hijack our plane and bomb Cuba?" Jerry asked.

"Maybe," Cynthia suggested, "maybe they wanted an excuse to increase Homeland Security."

"But why?" Jerry still didn't get it.

Cynthia shrugged. "Raise oil prices, political maneuvers."

"Oh," Bronze was silent.

"But he's the air marshal," Jerry reasoned. "He was supposed to be on our side."

"That made him the perfect accomplice to plant the bomb in the plane, to get by security and to pull off their little coup," Bronze said. "But something went wrong. Very wrong. Ms. Terrorist here decided that she wanted to change the agenda. Not refuel and fly to Afghanistan. She decided to bomb Cuba and take over for herself. Didn't you?"

"Sounds like Mr. Go to the Head of the Class just figured it all out, didn't you, honey? But do you know what happens now? Do you?" Mrs. Krutz just laughed. And everyone else just waited.

The Bomb

There was no difference in the smoothness of the flight as Mrs. Krutz hit a key on the keyboard and released a bomb over the water. No one would have noticed it had they not been holding their breath. Then there was a flash of light outside the window.

"What was that?" Cynthia asked.

"Damn," said Mrs. Krutz. "That wasn't supposed to happen."

"And what was that?" Bronze asked.

"Wrong target," Mrs. Krutz mumbled. "Maybe it's okay. Maybe it's better. Why the hell not?" and she laughed.

"What was the target supposed to be?" Bronze persisted.

"Wouldn't you like to know," Mrs. Krutz smirked.

The plane bucked and everyone had to steady themselves. It was impossible to see much in the darkness.

Taking sides

It seemed as if the seconds had lengthened. No one wanted to speak and yet everyone wanted to know what was going to happen.

Finally Mrs. Krutz gave a long and throaty laugh. "It's ridiculous!" She kept laughing.

Hackerstein was so angry he could not speak. He jammed his cell phone back in his pocket and started for the nearest door. "I need to use the toilet. That okay with you, Madam?" Hackerstein asked.

"Okay," said Mrs. Krutz. "Come right back."

Bill Bronze reached out and grabbed his arm. Hackerstein looked up and their eyes met. Bronze checked to see if Mrs. Krutz was watching and slipped out behind Hackerstein.

"You know she's nuts, don't you?" Bronze asked as he caught up with the air marshal. Hackerstein kept looking at Bronze's eyes. He finally nodded.

"And you know that she's lying about anything she promised you and anything she intends to do?"

Hackerstein nodded again.

"And she's probably lying or just plain ignorant because my guess is that if the government gave you a cell phone to use from the plane it probably works just fine," Bronze waited.

Hackerstein took out his phone again and was about to dial.

"Who are you going to call?" Bronze asked.

Hackerstein reflected quickly. How much should he tell the co-pilot?

"Your contact?" Bronze asked.

Hackerstein nodded.

"How much can you trust him?"

Hackerstein shrugged.

"If he hangs you out to dry then what?" Bronze asked. "Think! All our lives depend on this!"

"I'll call him," Hackerstein said under his breath. "I've got to give it a shot."

"Just be careful. He may just jerk you around. You may be as dispensable to him as you are to Mrs. Crazy Lady in there," he gestured towards the front of the plane.

Hackerstein dialed. They waited. Busy. He dialed again. Busy. Once more and, "Mr. Dylan? It's Hackerstein. We've got trouble." Pause. "I know you don't want to hear that; I don't want to say it. Mrs. Krutz, she's flipped. She won't honor the agreement." Pause. "How do I know? She just turned the plane around. She says we're not going to Afghanistan." Pause. "What do you mean, 'other contengencies'? What do you mean 'other contingencies'? She's flipped. She wants to bomb Cuba. The lights are out." Pause. "Well, there are some things you may not know. Why don't you 'check out your sources' and call me back." Pause. "Yes, yes, I can call again. I'll call in 10 minutes." He stuffed the phone in his pocket and wiped his forehead with the back of his hand.

"Good man, Hackerstein," Bronze said. He looked around and grabbed two small bottles of scotch from the beverage cart. He opened one for himself and opened one and handed it to Hackerstein. They both finished the tiny bottles in one swallow. And they both took a couple of deep breaths.

On the house

"Would you like a complementary beverage?" Cynthia Billings asked Olivia Livingston and her daughter Karen.

"Don't you dare take a drink," the elderly passenger threatened her grown daughter.

"Mother!" Karen protested. "You know I don't drink!"

"We have ginger ale, diet cola, orange juice, cranberry juice, seltzer," Cynthia offered.

"Under the circumstances I think it's only fitting that you offer us something!" the dowager asserted.

"What are the circumstances, Mother?" Karen asked.

"I am not a simpleton! I am not feeble!" Olivia raised her voice. "I know full well what is going on!"

"And what is that, Mother?" Karen asked. She smirked and waited to see what her mom would come up with.

"There is a malfunction on this plane," Olivia said in an even tone. "We are undergoing severe technical difficulties, so serious that the pilot is afraid to speak of them openly because he might panic some of the weaker passengers." Olivia was very proud that she had figured this out.

"And?" Karen continued.

"And therefore we are being given a peace offering to simultaneously soothe our nerves and quiet our suspicions," Olivia nodded solemnly.

Karen exchanged glances with the stewardess.

"Well?" Olivia said. "Am I wrong?"

"I am really not at liberty to say," Cynthia gave Karen a knowing nod, "but you are correct that the pilot does not want the passengers alarmed unduly. And he wants you to be as comfortable as possible."

"Under the circumstances," Olivia put in, nodding twice. "There! Didn't I tell you?"

Karen sighed. "Under the circumstances I would like a white wine," she said and patted her mother's arm appreciatively.

Further friendships

"Stewardess! Scotch rocks, please," said Mike Nolan motioning Cynthia Billings over. "And for you?" he asked Kathy Spruce.

"I don't—" she hesitated.

"Oh, come on! Be a seasoned traveler! Here's something to tell the folks back home! Don't say you didn't live it up!"

Kathy shrugged, slightly embarrassed. "Well—"

"That's more like it! Brandy for the lovely lady!." Mike made a grand gesture in the air and laughed. Kathy smiled.

"How far out of the way is all this taking us?" he asked as Cynthia poured the drinks.

"I can't guess," Cynthia said with her eyes averted. She passed Kathy her glass with a napkin and a bag of snacks.

"I mean are we going to make our connecting flights or what?" Mike persisted.

"All possible steps are being taken to avoid any inconvenience with respect to other airlines," Cynthia smiled thinly, glad the cabin was dark.

"You mean you'll call ahead and tell the other flights we're delayed?" Kathy asked as she took a sip of her brandy. She was not accustomed to drinking and made a face. Mike nudged her and smiled.

"Something like that," Cynthia nodded, handing Mike his scotch.

"Does this happen often?" he asked the stewardess.

Cynthia shrugged. "There are often problems with the flights," and then she stopped. She didn't want to sound like flying with her airline was a routinely hazardous experience. "Things come up," she said, hoping that would end it.

Then the plane bucked forward. The drink cart with all the bottles and beverages trembled. The passengers had their drinks sloshing around, some spilling. There was a general intake of breath and exclamations of "Oh!" and "Ah!"

Cynthia felt she was on the verge of crying. She took a couple of deep breaths.

"Mike!" Kathy exclaimed and seized his arm. He put the arm around her and kissed the top of her head.

"Here," he said, handing her his napkin to sop up her spilled brandy.

The lucky dog

"Stewardess," Candy Krauss called out. "Do you have anything for my dog? He's getting very frightened." And it was true. Little Doggo, the therapy dog, was needing a bit of therapy himself. "I'm so glad you are here with Mama," she crooned at him and squeezed him tightly.

"Would you like a complementary beverage?" Cynthia asked.

"White wine," Candy said. "Make that two white wines, just so you don't have to come back again."

"You've got the right idea," Zedda Stein piped up. "Eat, drink and be merry, for tomorrow—" she paused dramatically.

"How awful!" Candy said, hugging Doggo again.

"I'm sorry if I frightened you," Zedda continued. "Zedda Stein," she held out her hand.

"Candy Krauss," Candy took her hand. "And this is Doggo. Doggo, shake hands with the nice lady." Doggo shivered and sniffed Zedda's outstretched fingers. Then he shook hands.

Zedda smiled appreciatively.

"Vodka," said Zedda to Cynthia. She turned to Candy. "You see, it's always in times of stress that a person's true character is revealed, for better or for worse." She nodded. Candy sipped away. "In past times we didn't have such dramatic occurrences like," she struggled for the right words, "mechanical failures that affected hundreds of people. You would have to have a war or a plague, to get the same degree of drama, but now it is more of a routine occurrence."

Cynthia nodded. She really didn't know what this woman was talking about.

"Man contemplates his mortality far more infrequently now than in the past. Now," Zedda took a big swallow of vodka, "we have movies, big blockbuster movies that we go to and watch the heroes and heroines face unbelievable dangers every ten minutes. And we transfer our sense of danger, of expectation of ending of life, to these characters. So we are, in a sense, living through them." She took another swallow.

"I like romantic movies," Candy said, "like Miss Congeniality and Miss Congeniality Two. Or comedies like Dog Show." She giggled. "Doggo likes Dog Show or any show with dogs and cats. Of course, he didn't like Mars Attacks where Jessica Parker gets her head put on the body of a Chihuahua. That's just gross. Doggo would never want the head of a human, would you, Doggo?" She hugged him again.

"Movies like The Hobbit or the Lord of the Rings trilogy express in a unique way the fusion of the Medieval forms of warfare with the modern computer technology, so we can actually see what it must have been like to fight and storm castles in the 14th and 15th centuries. So, in a way, these modern inventions enable us to understand the past better,"Zedda continued.

"I liked the dresses and jewelry in the first Lord of the Rings. Then they had too much of those drab peasant clothes," Candy smiled pleasantly, glad to be having a conversation about something she had some knowledge of with someone so much more experienced than herself.

"But always, there was, in the Middle Ages," Zedda continued, "the awareness of death so close. The Black Plague, for example, could kill you in 24 hours, so every day would be precious, a gift."

"Like the anthrax scares on the envelopes?" Candy asked.

Zedda swallowed more vodka. "Waitress?"she called. "I mean 'Stewardess'!" She needed another vodka.

Ten minutes later

"Here goes," said Hackertein dialing the cell phone. "Mr. Dylan?"

Bronze tried to catch a glimpse of how things were going from Hackerstein's face.

"You're still checking?" Hackerstein's voice rose sharply. "Can't you tell that our electric is out?" Pause. "Well, how long are we expected to wait?" He nodded his head. "You can't tell where we are? Don't you have some kind of tracking device?"

Bronze kept nodding to keep Hackerstein going.

"And what are we supposed to do in the meantime? She's already released a bomb but it was not the agreed upon target." Hackerstein waited. "I don't know what she hit but there was some light and the plane was affected. How long before she bombs something else?"

Bronze saw that Hackerstein was in danger of throwing the phone on the floor so he grabbed it out of his hand.

"Mr. Dylan, this is Bill Bronze, the co-pilot. Now I know you don't know me from Adam but I know something about flying a plane and unless we get some kind of ground contact here we're going to be in a great deal of trouble. Not only can we crash, and everyone on board will be killed, but the area we crash into will be destroyed. Innocent people, houses, cars and trucks will be incinerated. You'll have an international incident on your hands."

Now it was Hackerstein's turn to study Bronze's face.

"And how exactly do you suggest we proceed?" Bronze was trying to keep his voice down. "How much longer?" Pause. "Listen, can you at least patch us into some air traffic control to guide us down?"

Pause. "Yes, we will call back in 15 minutes." He handed the phone to Hackerstein.

"That was good, what you said about crashing into innocent people," Hackerstein said in a subdued voice.

Bronze nodded. He hoped that Mr. Dylan was not as cold hearted as he sounded.

Then the plane lurched forward again.

The storm

"We're all going to die!" Ethiopia Beldez screamed as the plane lurched and her drink spilled into her lap.

They were flying into what seemed to be a hurricane. Screams rang out from others as the hail on the wings became larger.

"It's going to crash!" Enid Snark yelled. "I saw it on the weather channel."

"That's hail! It can't be a hurricane!" said Mike Nolan.

Cynthia Billings tried to calm some of the passengers down but the chaos was spreading as the plane was tilting from side to side.

"What's going on? Who's in charge?" Mr. Lovehill yelled. "My family is on board here!"

Bill Bronze stepped up to the front of tourist class.

"Ladies and gentlemen, I am the co-pilot. You can see we're having a bit of turbulence—"

"Cut the crap, man!" Buster Walker called out.

"That's exactly what I'm trying to do, young man," Bronze continued. "And you yelling doesn't help matters." He pulled Hackerstein aside. "Tell him that he will panic the women and children," Bronze said.

Hackerstein went over to Buster Walker and whispered in his ear.

"Ladies and gentlemen," Bronze continued, "please fasten your seat belts. We need you to remain calm. The best thing you can do right now is to stay in your seats so that we don't unbalance the plane further. We're have to get through this rough patch of turbulence before we can reach our destination." He tried to see the result of his words and luckily the commotion among the passengers seemed to dissipate.

"Come on, Hackerstein," Bronze said. "Let's see what's doing up front."

Chaos

Up front was a scene of tension and despair. Mrs. Krutz was still trying to fly the plane, but not very successfully.

"For god's sake, let Stark take over!" yelled Jerry, the cop.

"Over my dead body!" Mrs. Krutz snapped.

"That's just what's going to happen!" yelled Jerry.

"Come on! Be reasonable!" Talenkov argued.

"The hail is getting in the engines," Bronze reasoned. "You've got to compensate."

"Compensate my ass!" Mrs. Krutz snarled. "I don't care if we all go down right now."

"But what about your grand mission, Ms. Hole in One? Don't you want to inflict more damage?" Bronze baited her.

That seemed to have an effect.

"Alright. But no funny stuff." Mrs. Krutz set up the computer to let the pilot take over the controls. "Remember I can launch the other bomb any time I want to."

Jerry looked at Bronze. "Maybe we can make a grab for it," Jerry whispered.

"I heard that!" Mrs. Krutz turned violently. She slammed her laptop shut.

"Great," said Bronze. "That went well."

Back with the passengers

"This is terrible! We're all going to die!" screamed Mrs. Mira Solaris.

Cynthia Billings went up to her. "If you can just calm down, Madam."

"How can I be calm? Our daughter is dead! We're going to her funeral and now this happens!"

"If you just—" Cynthia started, when she saw that Mr. Solaris was clutching his chest. "Sir, are you alright?"

"My arm," he said. "I can't breathe."

"Is there a doctor on board?" Cynthia called out.

Suddenly Dr. Wendy Lee stepped over the aisle and was at her side. She felt Joseph Solaris' pulse.

"Do you have any heart medicine?" she asked Mrs. Solaris.

"Oh, my god! I knew this would happen! He's having a heart attack!" Mrs. Solaris cried. "Joseph! Joseph!" She clutched his hand. "Do something! Do something!"

Dr. Lee leaned over Joseph Solaris and it looked like she was taking his pulse. She applied pressure there and to a point under Solaris's nose.

"Recline the seat, please," she said to the stewardess. Cynthia did so.

"Here," said Mira Solaris, offering Dr. Lee the pill bottle with Mr. Solaris's medicine.

The doctor put a tablet under his tongue.

"Take lots of deep breaths," Dr. Lee instructed. She turned to the wife. "You must be calm now for your husband. Do you understand?"

Mrs. Solaris nodded. Tears were in her eyes. "Thank you, Doctor! Thank you! I don't know how I can ever thank you!"

"Just keep him calm. And you keep calm too," she said.

"I don't know how you can remain so composed," Cynthia said to Dr. Wendy Lee.

"If I were not composed I would probably put the pressure in the wrong place," Dr. Lee said and they both laughed.

"That's amazing!" Buster Walker said to his wife. "Did you see that, honey? The doctor saved this guy's life!"

"Keep it down, please," Cynthia said. Buster and his wife both nodded.

There was a general buzz of subdued excitement and exclamations of "Wow!" and "Amazing!" as the news was relayed through the cabin. That did much to relieve the mounting fear as the plane lurched again.

General panic

"I can't stand this! We're all going to die!" screamed Ethopia Beldez. "It is God's judgment against us!"

"Hey, cool it, Lady!" came another shout.

"Please be seated," Happy Charles put a hand on her shoulder.

"It's the computers! God is showing how strong he is and how weak they are!" Ethiopia yelled.

"Please, Madam," said James Cologne. "I work with computers and computers are only as good as the people who work with them."

"Man is weak, God is strong!" she continued.

"If God didn't want us to have computers," James said slyly, "he wouldn't have allowed us to invent them."

"You got something there," said Buster Walker.

"Fools!" Ethiopia rang out. "You put your faith in the devil's machines!"

"Hey! Cut that out!" James protested.

"Madam, please! You're frightening the other passengers," Happy tried to ease her back into her seat. He looked for Cynthia to help him out.

"Allow me," said Buster Walker, and he reached over and touched a pressure point on Ethiopia's hand which immediately forced her back down.

She shook her hand as if to rid herself of the pain, but the brief jolt seemed to have its effect.

"Thanks, man," said Happy to Buster.

Cynthia rejoined them. "What's up?" she asked.

"My man," Happy referred to Buster, "just did some magic—"

"Elementary, My Dear Watson," Buster explained, "I just applied a little pressure to one of her pressure points. The kind of thing cops to do subdue criminals."

"And how would you know about that?" Mrs. Joline Walker asked.

"Never you mind, Sweet Cakes," Buster kissed her on the top of her head.

"Well, thank goodness for that special magic," Happy said.

"Yes," said Cynthia. Mr. Walker had just given her an idea.

The doctor is in

"Dr. Lee," Cynthia approached Dr. Wendy Lee. "Could you come with me, please?"

Dr. Lee stood up as Cynthia guided her into the rear galley.

"Is there a problem?" she asked.

Cynthia took a deep breath. "Yes, there is a big problem. You must keep this to yourself—" she began. She almost asked her to remain calm, but she realized that Dr. Lee's composure was part of the reason she turned to her. "We have a mad man up front. Actually it's a woman. She's flying the plane."

"What?" Dr. Lee was shocked.

"It's a long story, but she has effectively kidnapped the plane and we are off course. She's aiming to—" Cynthia wondered how much she should reveal. "She has an evil agenda to kill not only the passengers and the crew, but others on the ground as well. We can't get the controls away from her."

Dr. Lee nodded.

"Do you think you could," Cynthia swallowed, "do something that would paralyze her for a few seconds? Just long enough for the policeman who is in with the co-pilot to get the controls away from her?"

Dr. Lee considered.

"If the policeman gets near her she might suspect something. I know this must sound like I am talking crazy—" Cynthia continued. "It sounds like a movie plot."

Dr. Lee looked at Cynthia and took her arm.

"You would not come to me, a total stranger, if there were something else that you could do. I realize the plane is in danger, but I had no idea it was so serious. I will help in any way I can."

****

"Don't you think you should let a professional handle this?" Jerry asked Mrs. Krutz as the golf ball sized hail banged on the windows, making star shaped cracks.

"Shut up," Mrs. Krutz snarled from between her clenched teeth.

"The hail will get into the engines," Hackerstein yelled. "You must land the plane immediately!"

"Yeah! You'd like that!" Mrs. Krutz snapped.

The plane lurched again. The wind picked up and began to sway the plane from side to side. Mrs. Krutz tried to counteract the pressure by turning the steering mechanism strongly and in the opposite direction but she was no match for Mother Nature.

Those in the first class were continually slammed against one another as the plane bucked the storm.

Cynthia moved up front and took Jerry's arm.

"There's an emergency ," she said with anguish in her voice. "One of the passengers is having a heart attack," she whispered and she looked at Jerry, squeezed his arm and applied pressure. "It's serious. It could change everything."

Jerry was quick to react. "My arm!" he yelled. He clutched at his chest. "What's happening? I have pain in my arm! My heart!"

"He's having a heart attack!" Cynthia screamed. "Let me get the doctor!" She pushed by Mrs. Krutz as Jerry collapsed into a jump seat. She pulled Dr. Lee forward.

"Here's the patient," she said to her.

"Move him closer to the window so I can see," Dr. Lee said. Bronze lifted Jerry on the other side.

As Dr. Lee leaned over him the plane bucked again and he was thrown up against Mrs. Krutz. Dr. Lee quickly executed the paralyzing maneuver on Mrs. Krutz's neck; Mrs. Krutz was brought to the floor in pain. Bronze took the computer and fumbled around for the right key.

"How the hell—" he search. "Found it." He punched a couple of keys and turned control of the storm tossed plane back to Captain Stark. "Back on track."

"Thank goodness!" Cynthia Billings exhaled a sigh of relief. "Thank you, Doctor, thank you! We all thank you,"

"Amen to that," Jerry said as he slapped the handcuffs on Mrs. Krutz.

But their troubles were far from over.

Hackerstein's helpers

"Hackerstein," said Bronze, "aren't you going to call that contact of yours and see if they can guide us down?"

Hackerstein looked up. "Yeah," he said. "Just a minute."

"We don't have a minute," Bronze said. "At 600 miles per hour we don't have half a minute. Let's go." Bronze let Cynthia go first and he walked behind Hackerstein.

Before Hackerstein had gone two steps Bronze jostled him and twisted his arm behind his back.

"Grab the phone!" he called to Cynthia. She caught it as Hackerstein dropped it. "Hit redial! Here, give it to me!" Bronze took the phone as he gave Jerry charge of Hackerstein.

"Mr. Dylan," Bronze said loudly. "We need a ground contact to land this plane. We're in charge now, so forget Hackerstein, forget Mrs. Krutz. We are American citizens and unless you can talk us down, you will have a major scandal on your hands."

The passengers

Everyone was strapped in for a landing and trying to withstand the pressure of being tossed from side to side. The aircraft bucked the winds.

"There's no light down there!" Joline Walker yelled.

"Just hold tight, baby," Buster said as he laced their fingers together.

Ethiopia Beldez was throwing up into an airbag. Nor was she the only one.

Happy Charles was moving from row to row, like a bowling ball clattering down the gutter. The panic was greater than he had ever experienced, even when the plane he was in was forced to discharge passengers over the ocean. At least then it had been daylight and they had a PA system to give instructions. Now there was nothing. He didn't know what was happening with Cynthia. He began to take stock of his brief life.

"I wish I hadn't taken this flight," he thought. "Kind of late for that." He tried to make out anything outside the aircraft windows. "If I get out of this alive I will never take a single hour for granted," he swore to himself. "I'll cherish all my in-laws and thank the Lord for every day of my life. I will hug my mom like there's no tomorrow, because there might not be. I'll buy myself that expensive sweater I had my eye on. Every glass of water will taste like wine—and I will never take any single thing for granted."

"Brace for impact," Cynthia yelled. "Brace, Brace!"

The plane dropped lower. And lower. As if in slow motion, they began to feel a resistance under the plane; they were hitting treetops.

The hailstones continued, making a racket. The whirr of the engines was getting clogged. Fire broke out on the wings.

"Fire! Fire! the wings are on fire!" someone called out. There was general panic.

People rose up out of their seats. They grabbed their bags. Several opened the overhead bins to get their carryon luggage.

"Oh, my god!" a woman wailed. "Oh, my god!" Her exclamation could barely be distinguished against the crying and screams.

"Keep your seats!" Happy Charles directed. "If we have to land you will have time to evacuate the aircraft, but if you stand up now you will unbalance the plane!" He hoped he sounded more convincing than he felt. He knew that they were going to crash and it was just a matter of minutes.

The rain and the hail counteracted the fire on the wings. The body of the plane slammed forward, taking the tops of trees with it. There was an open field. The plane ground to a halt, crashing the nose into more trees on the further end.

Branches broke through the windows. Pieces of metal and glass were flying all over. Everyone was screaming, some were crying. The body of the plane was vibrating. The noise of the thud as the plane hit was louder than any other sound.

"Unbuckle your seatbelts!" Happy Charles yelled as the plane slammed to a stop. He headed for the emergency exits. "Don't panic; everyone will get out!'

The overhead bins opened up and the contents fell on the passengers' heads. The oxygen masks dropped down like huge plastic spiders. There was crying and screaming.

Charles made it to the front of the plane and tried the first door, but it was jammed against a palm tree outside. He had better luck with the second door. There was rush of air as the cabin depressurized.

"Evacuate!" he yelled. "Evacuate!"

He let out the plastic landing chute for landing over water and tried to guide the passengers towards it.

"Easy does it; just slide down," he said. Some of them had life jackets on. Others were clutching their carry bags and purses. There were bloody faces . There was crying and wailing.

"Evacuate!" Charles instructed. "Forget your luggage! Whatever you stop to take could cost someone their lives!"

"Oh! My god!" Mrs. Solaris moaned. "Help me with Joseph! Please! He's had a heart attack!" James Cologne took Mr. Solaris's arm and wrapped it around his neck. He guided him to the exit.

"I can't do this! I can't!" Olivia Livingston complained.

"Shut up, Mother," Karen snapped as she pushed the older woman down the chute.

"Doggo! Doggo! Let us out!" Candy Krauss called out.

"After you," Zedda Stein said sarcastically as she clutched her tote bag to her breast.

"After you," said Sunny Sanchez to Holly Nash. She smiled at him gratefully.

"And you couldn't stop this, Miss Goddess of the Mandrake Wold?" Lucy Wardhope said to her daughter.

"Shut up," said Aunt Ethel and she pushed herself off the plane as quickly as the crowd would allow.

Touching the ground

Just then the right wing broke off. It had been held up in some branches and the fire from the wing burned the trees until the branches could not hold the weight of the wing. The fire began to spread to the vegetation. An eerie red glow lit the scene against the horizon. What the smoke obscured was ghastly with bits of metal and glass from the crash being thrown in all directions. The heavy rain kept the fire contained but made the ground slippery.

The debarked passengers began to run away from the wreckage as fast as possible. All feared the explosion of the gas if the fire got to the engine.

"Cover your noses and mouths!" Happy Charles counseled. Cynthia had taken a gallon of water and was handing out napkins from first class soaked with water so that the passengers could breathe more easily.

As pieces of the plane hit nearby bushes, branches caught fire. With each new outbreak of flames there were more screams and more panic.

What was missing were the sounds of sirens and ambulances.

"Where are the rescue workers?" Buster Walker asked. He had a protective arm around his wife and was guiding her away from the remains of the plane.

James Cologne tried his cell phone. "I can't get a signal," he called out. "Maybe it's the rain." Others began trying their phones.

"Help Mrs. Livingston," Cynthia said to Dr. Lee. She had guided Mr. and Mrs. Solaris off the plane. Now the elderly woman was leaning on her daughter Karen, but coughing alarmingly.

"Find Bill Bronze," Cynthia said to Happy Charles. "Get him to have Hackerstein use his cell phone." Happy looked at her quizzically. "It has a special government long range," she explained.

The controls

When the plane crashed, Herb Stark was at the controls. He had done the best possible job by engineering a landing without the benefit of the usual electrical system. The computer set up by Mrs. Krutz was not very sophisticated, but that worked to his benefit. There was not enough time to fine tune their descent.

Jerry had let Talenkov out of his handcuffs and placed them on Mrs. Krutz before she could react.   Jerry's partner Hank had charge of their prisoner, Sam Banks.

There were many with bleeding faces; several had arms hanging down at unusual angles. There were cries from the body of the plane. Not everyone had been able to get out.

"You two," Talenkov grabbed Mike Nolan and Frank James. "We got to get them out of the plane." He zipped up his leather jacket, put a wet bandana over his mouth and charged into the flames. The two men followed suit.

They emerged minutes later dragging women and men, Enid Snark and Cyd Sample among others, their arms around the rescuers' necks. All were coughing. Their faces were streaked with blood and rain.

"Where's Hackerstein?" asked Happy Charles when he reached Herb Stark.

Stark looked around. "I've been a little busy," he said.

"You did a great job, Captain," Happy said. "Cynthia said that Hackerstein has a special government phone that could get us some help."

Herb Stark laughed. "Let's hope," he said. He shielded his eyes and tried to find the slightly hunched form of Henry Hackerstein.

Unexpected heroes

James made an unlikely hero; although he was tall, he was of slight build.

"Be careful, " said Evangeline, giving him a quick hug.

"Anything you say, pretty lady." He smiled.

Going back inside the plane was anything but appealing. The smoke was thick, the flames starting to lick up the seats. It was difficult to make out anything.

"Yo! Man! Back here!" James followed the shouts to find Sunny Sanchez with Holly Nash who had passed out.

"You take her," Sanchez said. James realized that Sanchez's arm was bandaged by his coat.

"I'm so hot I caught fire a little more than I would have liked," Sunny quipped.

James picked up Holly's limp body and began to stumble toward the door of the plane.

"Wait! Wait! Don't leave me! Wait!" Ali Ashad called out.

James looked around. Ashad's white coat reflected the flames and made an eerie silhouette. He was pinned under several carry bags.

"Can you help?" James asked Sanchez. "Just throw the bags aside, but be careful; the handles might burn you."

Sanchez looked around for some cloth to wrap his good hand. He took the airline blanket that someone had left on a seat and bound up his hand.

"Easy does it," Sanchez said as he threw bag after bag off of Ashad.

"Come on, man! I can't breathe!" Ashad yelled.

Sanchez lifted him slowly. "Anything broken?" he asked.

"I don't know, I don't know! I can't breathe!"

"Take it easy. The more you panic the harder to breathe." Sanchez directed. He tore off a piece of the blanket and gave it to Ashad. "Breathe through this," he said. He put Ashad's arm around his shoulder and together they stumbled down the aisle.

"Hurrah! Our hero!" yelled the passengers when James emerged with Holly in his arms.

"Another hero!" they yelled as Sanchez rested Ashad on the ground. There was applause but it did not last long.

More for less

"I forgot my medication," Candy cried. "I took the wrong bag."

"Surely you can get a replacement once we get into a town," Cynthia reassured her.

"No, I took the wrong bag. I'm going to need it very soon. There isn't enough time. I feel so stupid."

"I'll go back," Sunny Sanchez interrupted. "What does the bag look like?"

"It's not necessary. It's too dangerous," Cynthia insisted.

"Please," pleaded Candy. "It's a red quilted bag with black and white flowers, about so big," she indicated ten inches. "I took this one instead," she showed him another floral bag. "It has the same pattern."

"Where would it be?" Sanchez asked.

"About seat number 16," Candy said. "I can't tell you how much—"

"It's okay," Sanchez said. "I've risked more for less."

Sanchez put a wet bandana over his mouth and forced himself to go back into the plane. He could hardly distinguish the seat numbers through the smoke. His foot hit something near where he imagined Candy had been sitting. There was a flash of light as the flames flared.

It was a black backpack but when he disentangled the strap from his foot something fell out of the overhead. A glance revealed the number 15 above the seat.

It was a soft quilted floral tote; he grasped it, stuck it under his arm and propelled himself out of the plane and onto the slide.

"Thank you, thank you," Candy said as he handed her the bag. She gave him a big hug and a kiss on the cheek.

"I hope the heat didn't damage the medicine," Sanchez said and coughed.

Candy revealed an inner pouch with a cold pack, all but melted. "Looks okay." she said skeptically. "Listen, you didn't have to do this." She looked at him so seriously and with such gratitude. Sunny had never been looked at like that, certainly not by his last girlfriend. He shrugged and tried to downplay it.

"You're my hero," Candy said.

"Really?" Sunny couldn't believe this.

"I'm serious. If I didn't have this medicine I wouldn't be able to function, not that I'm doing such a great job now."

"Looks fine from this man's viewpoint," Sunny said.

"I will think of you every time I don't have a nightmare," Candy said.

"The medicine does that?" he asked. She nodded.

"Maybe there are other ways I could help you sleep better," Sunny ventured.

"I hate having to rely on medicine," Candy continued. "Makes me feel like a drug addict."

"Not really," Sunny said.

"You have no idea. And when anything goes wrong with my health insurance or the pharmacy screws up—It's like a mini-miracle I could get enough to take on this trip. And then I go and forget it—" She was about to cry.

"Hey," Sunny put his arm around her and gave a squeeze. "It's okay now. Just take a deep breath."

Is it witchcraft?

Talenkov reentered the plane and followed the screams coming from inside the aircraft. The light from the flames made eerie shadows. The smoke billowed.

A body fell against his arm.

"Help me!' coughed Lucy Wardhope. Talenkov took her arm and put it around his neck.

"My niece, Nancy," Lucy whispered.

"Where?" Talenkov looked around.

Lucy pointed back inside the plane.

"Fainted," Lucy said.

"Here," said Talenkov and he gave her a damp kerchief to put over her mouth.

Talenkov shielded his eyes and listened. He started to drag Ms. Wardhope out of the plane when he stumbled across the feet of her niece, The Goddess of the Mandrake Wold. He put Lucy into a seat, grabbed The Goddess and pushed her upright.

"You first!" he directed as he jostled Ms. Wardhope towards the door. When he had gotten half way he hurried back for Nancy.

The smoke was so intense it was almost impossible to see. "Nancy!" Talenkov called out. "Nancy!" Again his foot hit something. She was on the floor, limp. And there was another body next to her, a man.

The man reached up and grabbed Talenkov's pant leg. He would not let go.

"Women first," Talenkov said.

"I'm Helmut Hardcastle," the celebrity whispered. "Please."

Talenkov pulled Helmut upright and propped him against a seat. Pulling Nancy with one arm across her body in a rescue hold, Talenkov reached Lucy Wardhope.

"Quick!" he commanded as he pushed Lucy in front of him.

Stark was at the door of the plane and he took Lucy. Talenkov reemerged still holding on to Nancy and Stark guided her also out of the plane.

Talenkov went back in for Helmut. Again he could not see the man and the crackling of the flames combined with screaming made it impossible to hear any individual cry for help.

He was coughing now but he persisted. His iron will had served him well in his chosen profession and it served him now.

He found the TV host collapsed and barely breathing. Just then part of the ceiling dropped in front of them, burning the seats it fell on. Talenkov's jumped as his jacket caught fire. He shook it off immediately and threw it into an empty seat.

Helmut's shirt and pants had caught fire. Talenkov stomped on his burning jacket until the flames were out, picked it up with singed fingers and wrapped Helmut in it. He rushed him from the plane.

When Talenkov could breathe again he cherished the air. He handed Helmut to Stark and wrapped his bandana tightly around his singed fingers to staunch the blood and stop the throbbing.

More rescues?

"Oh, my god!" Zedda Stein called out.

Candy Krauss and Doggo were standing next to her; Candy was coughing and petting Doggo.

"Where are the ambulances?" Enid Snark asked the captain. "When are they coming?"

"Soon, I hope," said Stark.

"Take it easy, honey," Buster Walker said to Joline. She was crying and limping while he supported her.

The Lovehill family had all survived, although Honey had injured her arm. The kids' faces were smeared with blood.

The sounds of the crackling flames and the snap and pop of the fire were only broken by the wailing of the survivors. Talenkov, Mike Nolan and Hank James were on their third trip into the plane when the body collapsed.

"Run!" Talkenkov yelled as the plane exploded. Everyone dove for safety.

Mrs. Krutz's refusal

While Talenkov, Mike Nolan and Hank James performed their heroic rescues, Jerry was left at the front of the plane with Mrs. Krutz.

"Okay, Lady, time to go," Jerry took off the handcuffs and pulled the terrorist roughly.

"That's what you think, Copper!" she yelled and broke free.

"In case you hadn't noticed, this plane is burning. If we don't leave now we'll both go up in flames! Is that what you want?"

Mrs. Krutz's laughter would have petrified the most hardened horror buff. "You think you know everything! That's what's wrong with the current generations. They have no thought for the long view! It's instant gratification! The remote control rules!"

Jerry was looking back and forth, seeing the panicking passengers back lit by the flames outside the window. "We don't have time for this."

"If not now, when?" she kept laughing. "You think I'm the only one? You think I'm alone in this? If I die twenty more will take my place! And you think this ends it! More explosions are on the way! You haven't ended something, you've just started it! Retaliation! You don't know the meaning of the word!"

"You're the one that crashed the plane, Lady! We're not the bad guys here!" Jerry yelled. He started coughing with the smoke.

"You've corrupted our world with all your electronic pathways! No one relates anymore! Everyone just wants quicker and more sophisticated gadgets. Let them be without electricity! God said 'Let there be light!' He didn't say 'Let there be electricity!' See what it's like when the lights go out all over!"

"Lady!" Jerry made a grab for Mrs. Krutz's arm, but she retreated further into the front of the plane. As he tried to reach her the top of the plane caved it and pinned her between the cockpit door and the crushed wall.

"You will die in darkness! Spiritual and material darkness! You will curse the day electricity was invented! You will—!" and the rest of her voice was consumed by screams as the flames engulfed her.

Jerry put up his forearm to avert the falling wreckage and ran to escape from the plane.

Hackerstein's revenge

Hackerstein had been among the first to deplane. He had retrieved his cell phone from the unwary Bronze when he bumped into him. He ran into the woods and immediately dialed Mr. Dylan. The line was busy. He kept dialing to no avail. After five minutes he put the phone inside his pocket. He had to face it. He was being cut off. The government either wanted nothing to do with him or the situation that had gone so far wrong from what they had outlined.

"Wasn't there some kind of backup plan?" he asked himself, trying to remember what had gone down what seemed like years ago. He was supposed to get on board, follow Mrs. Krutz's lead. They were supposed to threaten but not actually bomb anyone or anything. He and his wife were supposed to get a tidy sum for her medical expenses and his retirement.

Everything had unraveled. "I trusted her! I trusted her! How could I have been so naïve?" he thought. But then again, he was not the only one. The government had been fooled also. Mr. Dylan, who surely had so much more experience than himself, had been fooled.

Or had he? Had they known all along? Did the government have a hidden agenda? Had they purposely picked an unstable woman, a terrorist so much more unreliable— Here he had to stop his thoughts. "A reliable terrorist?" he laughed a dry, sarcastic laugh. What had he been thinking? Or had he been thinking at all? In his panic to save his wife and himself he had rushed into this. And now what would become of them? True, he had gotten off the plane with his life— something that was not to be made light of. Others no doubt had not been so lucky. And clearly the government wanted nothing more to do with them.

Would there be charges brought against him? Would he go to jail? Should he run further into the woods? For someone who had always "played by the rules" he had picked the wrong time to go against his basic nature. He was lost in more ways than one.

Friends in the neighborhood

The rain had tapered off, but the wet ground did have some effect on the burning plane, slowing the spread of ground fire.

"Some vacation, huh, Baby?" Buster Walker said as he kissed the top of his wife's head.

"Just glad we're alive," Joline replied, and coughed.

"You got that right," he smiled at her and kissed her again.

"I don't understand! How could the airline have allowed this to happen?" Lucy Wardhope fumed.

"Lucy, give it a rest," said Aunt Ethel. She was pressing a wet compress to the head of Nancy, aka Goddess of the Mandrake Wold. "You should be thanking the nice gentlemen who rescued your niece."

"I did, I did," Lucy said.

"He needs more help than I can give," Talenkov said to Herb "Be Right" Stark, indicating the prone form of Helmut Hardcastle, his body wrapped and bleeding.

"We need an ambulance!" Enid Snark snapped. "Where are the medics?"

"I guess the same place as the air traffic controllers: on vacation," said Buster Walker.

"Where are we anyhow?"

"My guess is the Bahamas," said Stark.

As the passengers lucky enough to have survived the crash commiserated, through the sounds of crying, moaning and the snap of the flames came the welcome wail of an ambulance.

"Horray! The cavalry has arrived!" someone yelled as the medics emerged from the rescue vehicle. Then there were the local police cars and two fire trucks from neighboring towns.

"I thought the police in the Bahamas would be black," said Mrs. Walker.

"I guess we got the left over white ones," said her husband.

Out of one of the vehicles came medics with pallets of water bottles and stretchers. Stark directed them to the injured and the rest of the crew passed out water and blankets.

"Boy, are we glad to see you folks," Stark said. There were many voices of assent.

"We're just glad we got here in time," said a tall, red headed medic. "There's another storm front moving in and it's causing lightning. There are ground fires."

Stark hoped that not too many had heard this. He looked around for Hackerstein, but in the darkness and the surrounding trees, it was impossible to see.

"Happy," he grabbed Happy Charles' arm, "see if you can find the air marshal, Hackerstein."

Happy looked at him quizzically.

"Where is Cynthia?" Stark asked.

Happy gestured towards of the fire vehicles.

"Cynthia!" Stark called as he ran towards her. "Have you seen Hackerstein?"

"No, " she said.

Stark cornered Mike Nolan. "Go with her," he indicated Cynthia, "and find the air marshal."

"But I'm needed here," Cynthia objected. "I can't leave now."

"We have the situation, as it is, under control," Captain Stark indicated Sherriff Lockwood and the ambulance personnel.

"I can't go just now," Cynthia pleaded. "I don't want to go into the forest at night," she explained.

Stark considered.

"I can't, I just can't," Cynthia was on the verge of tears.

" Nolan, do you know what air marshal Hackerstein looks like?"

Mike Nolan shook his head.

"The guy passing out drinks along with Cynthia," Stark explained.

"Not really," said Nolan.

"Cynthia," Stark put his arm around her shoulder, "just go with Mike here. I'm not asking you to explore the whole forest. Just go around the edge and see if Hackerstein is around. If you don't find him in 25 minutes you come back. Okay? There won't be too many people wandering around in the dark. Take this flashlight," Stark continued, "and if you run into trouble come back sooner."

Cynthia nodded rapidly, holding back her tears. She exchanged glances with Stark. Nolan, along with most of the passengers, had no idea of what had gone on at the front of the plane.

The search party

"I'm really glad you're coming with me," said Mike Nolan, "because I really haven't a clue as to what this guy looks like. I didn't want to really say that because I didn't want to look stupid. Maybe it's because we are all so terrified and it's hard to focus. But, hey, I'm a guy. I'm supposed to be the strong one,"

"Don't be ridiculous," said Cynthia blowing her nose. "I mean we're all just out of our minds with worry here. How many of us have ever been in this situation before?"

"Well, you have a better chance of being hijacked," said Nolan. "You fly all the time."

"Not anymore," Cynthia admitted. "This was supposed to be my last flight."

"Uh-oh," said Nolan. "I guess I said the wrong thing."

"No, no, it's all right. I just keep thinking, 'What if I had handed in my retirement letter a week back ?' Or a month back? There's so much I still want to do. I had just started thinking of taking some courses in night school. You know, the kind of thing I usually can't sign up for because of my job. The classes don't start till next week. I thought I had timed it right. But if I had stopped before then I wouldn't be in this mess and—" She started crying.

"I'm so sorry," Nolan said. He shifted the flashlight to his other hand and put his arm around her. "It's okay. You'll still get a chance to take those classes."

She cried harder.

"I'm really batting a thousand here," Nolan said. He gave her a squeeze. "Hey, lucky we're not finding anything in these woods. We would be prime target for an angry bear, now wouldn't we?"

Cynthia laughed in spite of herself. She blew her nose loudly.

"That's right, bears don't like loud noises."

They both laughed.

"Can you shine the flashlight in my purse? I need another tissue," Cynthia said.

"What do you keep in here?" Nolan asked as Cynthia took out a high heeled shoe.

"That's my dress pump," she said. "I packed them in my luggage because I was going to celebrate my retirement when we got to Nassau. Then after the explosion I found this on the ground."

"Just one?" Mike asked.

Cynthia nodded.

"I guess that makes you Cinderella."

Cynthia blew her nose again. "It's really kind of gruesome."

"Maybe you'll find the other one later," Mike suggested. They trudged onwards.

"Damn!"

"What happened?" Cynthia asked as the beam from the flashlight disappeared onto the forest floor.

"Tripped over a root. No, it's okay. I'm not hurt. Just help me up a little here."

"Let me dust you off. Here, give me the flashlight."

"Sure. Well, that about does it for me. Let's head back. At least we're out of the range for the noxious fumes from the plane, right?"

Lost in the woods

Hackerstein was not the most resourceful of souls. On car trips he had always relied on his wife.

"You want to know where we are so much, you ask!" was his common retort.

He seldom went anywhere by himself. His work took him to all manner of cities, but all he had to find was the airport. Alone in the woods with night falling, he literally didn't know where to turn. He had not bothered to look for any landmarks when he left the burning airplane. He was so focused on reaching Mr. Dylan by phone he did not bother to think about what would happen afterwards.

In his rush to disappear from the sight of the airline crew, he had double crossed himself. He could not even see any light from the flames. What seemed to be a sky with enough light became patches of light between black branches. And then less and less light. The dark shapes of the trees all looked the same and there were no marked paths. As his predicament began to sink in so did the cold chill of fear.

He had no food, no water. "Help!" he shouted, to no avail. "I'll just pick one direction and walk that way," he said to himself. And, of course, he chose wrong. He headed deeper and deeper into the forest.

He tried dialing the phone again, 911. All he got was a busy.

"What!" he exclaimed in disgust "Wouldn't you know? Government issue! Worthless!" He almost threw it away, but something stopped him. "Maybe in a few minutes they will get off the line," he tried to convince himself.

Meanwhile he was getting a chill. The plane had been unbearably hot, but now the opposite was true. In his haste to escape, he hadn't brought his briefcase or his coat.

"My fault again," he thought as he almost bumped into a tree. He'd have to be more careful and with the fading light he had to feel his way, step by step.

"Hello!" he called out with what he hoped was cheerful optimism. "Hello!" There was no response. He had not realized how quiet the night could be. Always in a city or an airport or in traffic, he took background noise for granted and just blocked it out. There was nothing like that here. Instead of welcoming the velvet silence, it sounded to him like a black vacuum sucking out the air and leaving emptiness and death.

Talenkov on his own

Having supervised several successful rescues, Talenkov looked around for the missing Hackerstein.

"That bastard was responsible for all this, " he fumed."Captain," he said to Stark, "I'm going to find Hackerstein."

"Good luck," said Bronze. "That guy knew to get when the getting was good."

"Do you want some help?" Stark asked. "I just sent Cynthia and Mike Nolan off in that direction," he indicated the dense woods to the left.

"No, I'll take it on my own," Talenkov smiled and gave a short nod.

"If you find them, direct them back here," said Stark.

Talenkov nodded. "Will do." He went off at a brisk trot in the other direction.

This was going to be easier than he had hoped. Of course, the plane crash was not in his plans but it served him well enough. Maybe even better. He had a chance to play the hero and get into everyone's good graces. This could only be helpful. The first choice, of course, was to be not remembered at all, but that had not happened. Now he had a legitimate reason to go after Hackerstein and carte blanche to be angry with him. There were many ways he could play the endgame. Talenkov always enjoyed improvisation.

When he had gone far enough from the plane so that he knew no one could make him out, he stopped and took the belt off his trousers. He unzipped the inner compartment and removed a fine wire about 18 inches long, his personal garrote. It had served him well on many previous occasions and it was going to help him on this job as well.

He listened. And Talenkov knew how to listen. First he screened out the sounds coming from the plane. Then he screened out the wind in the trees, the occasional insect, rustling leaves, a lizard underfoot. He breathed deeply and regularly until all he could hear was the sound of his own blood circulating in his ears. He advanced step by step. After every ten steps he stopped and listened again.

Then he saw it: a light far in the distance. He heard rustling of someone or some animal moving through the forest. He stopped and listened as the sound became closer and closer. He was not alone in the forest anymore.

An unlikely friend

"Hello!" called out Hackerstein as soon as he heard what he thought were footsteps. "I'm here! Hello!"

The sounds came closer and closer.

"Hello! Hello!"

Suddenly he felt an hand on his arm.

"Sorry to startle you, buddy," said a man's voice. A flashlight shone on Hackerstein's face and blinded him.

"Who are you?" Hackerstein asked.

"I was doing some hunting and I heard you calling out," the man said. "Don't mind saying that you scared any game that might be around." He gave a rough laugh.

"I am so glad to see you," Hackerstein began to breathe normally. "You see I was in that plane that went down and I kind of lost my way."

"I'll say," said the man. "You're a distance from any form of human contact out here." He laughed again. "Don't worry; I'll take care of you."

"Thank you so much," Hackerstein said. "I was really starting to get worried. I mean, I'm not a woodsman by any means and I had no way of getting back to the plane, or getting anywhere, for that mattter." Then he cursed himself for mentioning the plane. Getting back to the plane was the last thing he wanted to do. "Maybe you can take me somewhere safe where I can make a phone call."

"Sure thing, buddy," said the woodsman. "Follow me. Just hold on to my coat." And he lead Hackerstein slowly through the forest.

They walked and walked. Hackerstein couldn't see any light from the burning plane, which was reassuring. Maybe he was getting lucky after all.

"What did you say your name was?" Hackerstein asked.

"I didn't, Henry," said the man.

"How do you know my name is Henry?" Hackerstein was suddenly afraid.

"I was sent to find you," the man said.

"Oh, the pilot is certainly resourceful," Hackerstein breathed a little more easily.

"Not exactly," said the man. "The pilot didn't send me."

"The airline?" Silence. "The local officials?" Hackerstein guessed.

"Wrong again." The man stopped and turned around. He blinded Hackerstein with the flashlight again. "Mr. Dylan sent me."

"Why that's wonderful!" Hackerstein gasped. They hadn't deserted him after all. This was better than he could have hoped. Now he could get back to his wife without dealing with all those pesky questions about Mrs. Krutz and the bombing. "But how did you find me?"

"Followed the tracking device in your phone," was the answer.

"What happens now?" Hackerstein asked.

"Now it's your turn to join Mrs. Krutz," said the man.

Hackerstein laughed. "I guess you didn't hear; Mrs. Krutz died in the wreckage. It's just me now."

"Not for long, Henry. Not for long."

And Henry Hackenstein heard the unmistakable racking of a double barreled shotgun.

Wonderful rescuers

"Take her over there," Stark said to Sanchez, indicating Candy Krauss. Her shoulder was bleeding. Sunny showed her to the area the emergency medics had set up for the wounded. She was still clutching Doggo.

"It's nothing," she protested. The sweat of being near the flames congealed on her skin like moist ice.

"Don't be brave," Sanchez said guiding her to a medic who looked like she had a minute to spare. "It always comes back to bite you later." His arm had been bandaged and he had been given some pain medication.

Candy smiled.

"Here, have some water," Sanchez said as he handed her a fresh bottle. "Wish I could offer something stronger."

"This is just fine," Candy said. "Athough an ice cold ginger ale would sure hit the spot."

"I was looking forward to those tropical margaritas," Sanchez said, "sitting by the beach with a bathing beauty like yourself in your bikini. Applying the suntan lotion," he winked at her.

"Guess I'm not the picture of island glamour at the moment," Candy said.

"From where I stand you look plenty glamorous," Sunny said as he pushed a strand of hair out of her eyes. She looked up at him. Doggo barked.

"Hey, no one's forgetting you," Candy said, squeezing the small traveler. She kissed him on the top of his head.

"How about some sugar for this little pup," Sunny said in a low voice. Slowly Candy put her free hand on his cheek.

"Need some help here!" Stark called out, breaking the mood.

There were more dead that the neighboring police and firefighters had pulled out of the wreckage. They were laying side by side in rows that kept getting longer.

Enid Snark was crying. "It's so ironic," she said between sobs. "Here I am, an old foggy, and there they are, some of them their lives just beginning. Now they'll never—" She kept sobbing.

Ethiopia Beldez put an arm around her shoulder.

Holly Nash had been treated for smoke inhalation, as had many others. James Cologne was standing next to her.

"Bet you never guessed you were getting on the Flight to Hell," he said to her. She just shook her head.

"We're going to put some of the passengers up in nearby motels," said the local sheriff, George Lockwood, to Stark. "The more serious cases will go to the hospital here and in the next town."

Stark nodded. It was already dark and the only light came from the emergency vehicles, the rotating red, white and blue lights like misplaced Christmas decorations. If you didn't look closely you would not make out the rows of the dead. You could still smell the smoke heavy in the air. The quiet of the surrounding forest absorbed the cries and moans of the survivors. The chill of the night had begun to moderate the heat from the plane.

And more rescues

"I tell you I can't move my legs! They're broken!" Olivia Livingston screamed.

"Take it easy, Mother. If your legs were broken you couldn't be standing." Karen said.

"I'm not! I'm dying! I'm dying!"

"Yes, Mother. You used to say from the moment we're born we start to die," Karen quipped.

"If I had a knife I would slit your throat," Olivia seethed. Karen guided her to one of the portable seats the rescue crew had provided.

"I'm dying! I'm dying!" Olivia persisted.

"Yes, Mother, we're all dying, except you're doing it much louder than anyone else," Karen said.

"Can I be of some help?" It was Dr. Lee, the acupuncturist.

"Oh, Dr. Lee." Olivia smiled. "I can't tell you how delighted I am to see you. Ever since you saved Mr. Solaris from his heart attack you have been my personal hero."

"What seems to be the problem?" Dr. Lee asked.

"It just hurts everywhere," Olivia whined.

"Well," said Dr. Lee, "that's to be expected when you are propelled down a chute from an airplane that has just crashed. We are all a little shaken up." She took her pulse. "Hmmm," she said.

"Am I all right, Doctor? How ill am I?" Olivia looked up at her.

Dr. Lee picked up her right wrist and dropped it. She did it with the other wrist. "Can you lift your left leg?" she asked.

Olivia obliged.

"And the right," Dr. Lee prompted.

Again Olivia obeyed.

"Turn your head this way," she had her follow her index finger. "And back." She turned her head back.

"I'm sorry to say that you have survived the crash most admirably," Dr. Lee said. "Not so many of the others." And she cast a glance at the dark row of what they all knew to be corpses.

For once Olivia Livingston was silent.

And more

"Please, I need to be in the ambulance with him," Mrs. Solaris said to the medic. Her husband was being loaded up. "He's had a heart attack," she explained.

"Of course," the medic gave her a hand up.

"Can I get some water here for my wife?" Mr. Franklin called out loudly. "I know it's not an emergency, but—"

One of the rescue personnel handed him a bottle. Billy Franklin unscrewed the top. "Here, dear," he handed it to Topaz Franklin.

"Has anyone seen Captain Stark?" Franklin called out again. There were murmurs and a hand tapped him on the shoulder.

"Captain Stark here," Stark smiled briskly. "What can I do for you?"

"Well, Captain, this may be nothing," Franklin began.

"Go on," Stark tolerated the man.

"But I saw that man in the handcuffs heading off into the woods," Franklin concluded.

"What man in handcuffs?" Stark's ears pricked up.

"You know, the prisoner, the one that was in first class. I noticed when he got off the plane and I was wondering how he was going to guide himself down the chute, but he did a pretty decent job of it."

"And?" Stark prompted him.

"Well, he was standing around with the other man who was in charge of him."

"The policeman?" Stark asked.

"I guess so; I mean he wasn't in uniform, but I guess he was a cop. I mean, he had the criminal by the forearm. And he put him down, sat him down, next to one of the ambulances while he, the cop, was helping various people out of the plane and directing them to the medics. And then when I looked up again I saw that the man in handcuffs wasn't there anymore."

"How long again was this?" Stark asked.

"Well, maybe 10 or 15 minutes ago," Franklin answered.

"Shit," said Stark between his teeth. "Bronze?" he yelled. "Bronze? Double quick here." He turned to Mr. Franklin. "Thank you, sir, you've been very helpful." Stark began a hurried survey of the area for his second in command.

"Did you hear that, honey?" Billy Franklin turned to Topaz. "The Captain said I've been very helpful," and he nodded his head with satisfaction.

The escape

Sam Banks, aka The Convict, saw the plane crash as his "golden opportunity." Although still in handcuffs and still guided by Officer Hank, he knew he just had to wait for the right opening.

Down the chute from the plane was a cinch. And waiting at the emergency medic station was just the perfectly busy place to slip away.

He had cleverly pinched the handcuff keys from Officer Hank when he was being hooked up to leave the plane, but he kept the cuffs on so for all intents and purposes he was still in shackles.

He waited till Officer Hank was assisting some of the wounded and he took a fireman's long coat and draped it over his shoulders so his hands didn't show. He walked around the side and back of the rescue vehicles. He took off the cuffs. In the growing darkness and confusion, it was easy to escape unnoticed.

He loitered around the sheriff's vehicle just long enough grab a weapon. He had already discovered a flash light inside one of the pockets of the fireman's trench coat. What luck!

"Got to love those local yokels with their firearms," he said to himself.

Walking quickly so as to seem official and busy, but not quickly enough to raise suspicion he headed for the woods. He did not look back.

He had done well not to respond to any of the people around him in the plane. No one really looked at him or talked to him. He was tall and sturdy with long hair but no facial hair. His was not a memorable or remarkable face. Under the cover of darkness with everyone wanting help or helping, he could have probably taken a couple of bags of ready cash from a Brinks truck, if it had been in the area, and escaped without any notice.

Once in the forest he breathed more easily. He found a pack of cigarettes inside the coat and lit up. Geez, he hated long plane flights. He began to cough; guess the smoke in the plane had gotten to him after all.

The flames from the plane still lit the horizon behind him and he made off quickly in the opposite direction. Sure, Officer Hank would notice he was gone. And they would begin to look for him, but with the wounded and dying on their hands, they had bigger problems.

The ground was soggy under his feet. When there were pine needles the ground was like a spongy cushion.

"Hasta la vista, baby," he said and smiled as he vanished into the woods.

Search and search again

"Bronze, find Hank and tell him his convict has escaped, unless he already knows, which I doubt. Then you go with him. I've got to stay here to coordinate the rescue," said Herb "Be Right" Stark with not some small annoyance.

"Righto," said Bronze and he started to search quickly among the survivors for the policeman.

The third ambulance closed its doors and put on the siren.

"Doggo!" cried Candy Krauss as her therapy dog leaped out of her arms. She made a mad grab for him, but was unsuccessful. "Sunny!" she yelled for her new companion.

"Right here," he was at her elbow.

"Doggo's gone! The siren frightened him!" She pointed in the direction of the forest.

"I'll get a flashlight," Sunny said and approached one of the rescue personnel. "Here," he said as he returned. They headed off together.

"Doggo! Doggo!" Candy cried, her voice almost in tears. "This can't be happening!"

"We'll find him," Sunny reassured her. "He's just frightened with all the commotion. He won't go far; does he go into the woods? Does he run off much?" They were walking rapidly into the darkness.

"We live in a city! He's never been outside in a field for any period of time!" She squeezed Sunny's arm. "He's used to the noise of the city, but all this confusion—"

"It's okay. Doggo! Doggo!" Sunny said. "Do you have some of his treats? What do you do when he gets loose?"

Candy searched her pockets and her purse. "Here." She brought out a rather small packet of dog bones made of dog appetizing foodstuff. She rattled them.

"Keep calling," Sunny said. "Doggo!" He whistled. "Doggo!"

The smell of the burned chemicals of the plane, the metal and the plastic, dissipated and the cold, clear night air filled their lungs.

Finders keepers

"I had no idea," Hank said when Bronze told him of Sam Bank's escape.

"I kinda figured," Bronze said. "Stark wants me to help you find the sucker."

"Great," said Hank. "Which way?"

"Well, one of the passengers saw him go off there," Bronze pointed into the almost indistinguishable woods.

"Great," said Hank sarcastically. "Lead the way."

They walked rapidly away from the light of the flames and the ambulances. They walked until the sounds died away.

"Did you hear something?" Hank asked. They both stopped. It was like the faint trudging of footsteps on the fallen leaves of the forest floor.

"Turn off the flash," Bronze commanded. And they waited. The sounds seemed to be getting further away.

"This way," Bronze whispered. They walked as rapidly as possible while taking care not to bump into each other or any trees. They tried to be silent, not to alert Sam Banks to their presence.

They stopped again to listen.

Bronze pointed silently to the right. They proceeded even more slowly and more quietly.

More of Sam Banks

The convict, aka Sam Banks, was in high spirits as he left the scene of the crash. It couldn't have worked out better if he had planned it. And he had planned it. Well, almost. Someone smarter than himself, or at least more knowledgeable, had planned it.

After walking some distance he thought he heard a noise. He stopped, turned off his flashlight and listened. Yep, there was someone very close to him. He tried to let his eyes become accustomed to the darkness. There was a dark form getting closer and closer.

"Hello! Hello!" came a voice.

Banks put out his arm and took hold of the dark form ahead of him.

"Sorry to startle you, buddy," he said. He turned his flashlight on to Hackerstein's frightened face.

"Who are you?"

"I was doing some hunting and I heard you calling out. Don't mind saying that you sacred any game that might be around." He laughed.

"I am so glad to see you," said Hackerstein. "You see I was in that plane that went down and I kind of lost my way."

"I'll say. You're a distance from any form of human contact out here." He laughed again. "Don't worry. I'll take care of you."

"Thank you so much," Hackerstein said. "I was really starting to get worried. I mean, I'm not a woodsman by any means and I had no way of getting back to the plane, or getting anywhere, for that matter. Maybe you can point me somewhere I can make a phone call."

"Sure thing, buddy. Follow me. Just hold onto my coat."

"What did you say your name was?" Hackerstein asked.

"I didn't, Henry."

"How do you know my name is Henry?"

"I was sent to find you."

"Oh, the pilot is certainly resourceful."

"Not exactly. The pilot didn't send me."

"The airline? The local officials."

"Wrong again. Mr. Dylan sent me."

"Why that's wonderful! But how did you find me?"

"Followed the tracking device in your phone."

"What happens now?"

"Now it's your turn to join Mrs. Krutz."

"I guess you didn't hear; Mrs. Krutz died in the wreckage. It's just me now."

"Not for long, Henry. Not for long." And Sam Banks racked his double barreled shotgun.

Who gets there first?

Talenkov saw a light from a flashlight in the woods. He heard the two men talking. Someone was with Hackerstein. Someone who might help his victim? He crept closer. They were talking. More talking. And walking. Talenkov moved slowly and carefully in the direction that they were going.

More talking. Laughter. And then, the racking of the shotgun. Not a happy sound. Moving so swiftly he surprised even himself, he reached the two men. He pulled out the garrote. He lassoed the neck of the man with the gun. And pulled quickly and tightly.

The intruder struggled. But just briefly. Talenkov lifted the body which was thick and large, but not too heavy, off the ground as the body gasped its last. Then let the body drop. There was a silence.

"Thank you! Oh, you don't know how glad I am to—" Hackerstein exhaled.

Talenkov felt around Sam Banks' body and removed the flashlight. He shone it on Hackerstein.

"How did you know where to find me?" Hackerstein asked. And waited for an answer.

Talenkov was taking his time. "I would have found you anyhow, but glad that I found you alive."

"Yes! Oh, yes! On that we can agree!"

"Because," Talenkov paused and tried to select his words carefully, "because it is my job rather than this nobody, it is my job to kill you." He picked up the shotgun and aimed it at Hackerstein's chest.

****

Bronze and Hank were near enough to hear the thud of Sam Banks' body falling on the forest floor. They saw the flashlight trained on Hackerstein's face.

Bronze put a cautionary hand on Hank's forearm. They were close enough to make out the plumes of breath from Hackerstein. And then they saw Talenkov picking up the rifle.

"Freeze! Police!" Hank yelled and raised his gun aiming at Talenkov. Talenkov turned the shotgun in their direction and doused his flashlight.

There were sounds of scrambling. When Bronze turned his flashlight in the direction of the men, Hackerstein was gone.

"Oh, crap!" Hank said, turning around with his gun still ready to fire.

"You got that right," Bronze said and swiftly moved the flashlight in a circle.

They tried to hear any sounds. There was a scurrying and a thud as if someone were hit with a big stick. The shotgun? Bronze tried to train the light in that direction. They moved quickly in the direction where the two men had been standing.

And then Hank almost tripped over Sam Banks' body.

And more searching

"Doggo! Doggo!" Candy cried. "Here, Doggo! Here, baby! Come! Come!"

Sunny tried whistling. "Here, boy! Here!"

They were tramping through the forest, the sound of their own footsteps masking any other nearby sounds. Candy was glad she had worn comfortable shoes.

"What if an animal gets him?" Candy whined.

"We'll just have to get to him first," Sunny said optimistically.

"He's never done this before!" she wailed.

They tramped on.

"Is that an inlet?" Candy asked. The trees parted and the sky was lighter. "I didn't know we were so near the coast." The reassuring rhythm of the nighttime ocean contrasted sharply with their distress. The sound of the waves beckoned and they walked towards the shore.

"What if he got too near the water and drowned?" she whined.

"Don't say that. He's a smart dog," Sunny counseled.

"Doggo, Doggo," Candy called, walking forward. "Ouch!" she bumped her knee on something just at the shoreline.

Sunny was at her side. "It's a lifeboat," he said. "And there's something in it." He pulled the boat further onto the shore. "It's heavy."

As the boat tipped slightly a heavy form slumped inside. The night sky reflected on the water threw some light on the face of a dead body.

"Don't' look," he said to Candy but it was too late.

"Yuck!" she exclaimed. "Who is it?"

Sunny shook his head. "Haven't a clue. Maybe it's a lifeboat from a ship that was caught in the hurricane."

"That's right," Candy agreed. "We haven't been able to get any of the news or weather. We really are out of it." She clung to Sunny. "I feel a little sick."

"I told you not to look," he chuckled.

"You sadist!" she said.

"Do you want to throw up?" he asked.

"I wouldn't give you the satisfaction. You think girls are weak," she bucked up.

"Not at all. I used to throw up on a daily basis," Sunny admitted.

"Bulimic?" Candy asked.

"Try again." Sunny paused. "I did a lot of drugs. You never knew if you were really stoned unless you were throwing up." He laughed. "Sounds crazy, I'll admit."

"What made you stop?" Candy asked.

"Well," he hesitated. "I'm stopping now. I mean I've stopped several times in the past, but it didn't seem to stick. Something always went wrong and I needed to get high. Or something always went right and I needed to celebrate. There's always a reason when you're an addict. That's why when you were saying you are addicted to your medicine I can understand the feeling. Believe me, I know what it's like."

"How are you going to stop? Do you have to take something? Won't you go into withdrawal?"

"I don't know. Guess I'll have to see. I need some motivation."

"Like something to look forward to?"

"Or someone to care about," Sunny said. "You can't stop taking drugs to please someone but you can stop if you want your lives together to be better. A friend of mine quit smoking along with his wife and whenever either of them felt the urge to smoke again, they'd go into the bedroom and have sex."

"Sounds like they didn't have a job to go to," Candy said.

"Sounds like a lot of fun to me," Sunny admitted. "Sure you're okay?" he asked and he felt her nodding as he pulled her to him and kissed her. "Wedding and a funeral," he whispered. A warm breeze touched their faces. They kissed again.

"I could learn to like this," Sunny murmured.

"Me too," said Candy.

"What's that you said?" Sunny teased.

"I said 'Me too'!"

"But that would mean you'd have to stick around," said Sunny.

"So would you," Candy said between kisses.

"You'd have to give up your condo, the one you've been planning six feet under."

"Convince me," Candy hugged him closer.

Just then they saw flashlights coming from the forest behind them. It seemed like two people, but the light was so brief and far away it was hard to tell.

"Quiet," whispered Sunny. His arms were around Candy and he could feel her breathing on his neck.

They couldn't make out words, but the men were talking. There were sounds of a scuffle. They heard the sound of the shotgun being readied.

"Oh, my god!" Candy exclaimed. "Oh, my god!" A shiver went through her.

Sunny squeezed Candy and held her quiet.

Just then they heard a little yip and Candy felt something rub against her ankle.

"Doggo!" she called out, bent down and picked up the forlorn animal. "Oh, Doggo!" She felt his little tongue on her cheek. She hugged him and covered him with kisses.

"Shhh!" cautioned Sunny and pointed in the direction of the two men. They waited.

Which way?

"Uggh!" said Hank. He shone the flashlight on the dead body of Sam Banks.

"Well, I guess you got your man," Bronze said.

"Or someone else got him," Hank said, examining the body. "Looks like he's been strangled. With a garrote," he added.

"Not your normal hunting gear," Bronze said, looking around them for the killer.

"And why would someone else be looking for him? Here?" Hank was perplexed.

"Maybe he just walked into something nasty," Bronze suggested.

Hank shrugged.

Then they heard a shot. And another.

"Hackerstein?" they both said. And began to run as quickly as they could between the trees in the direction of the shots.

Sound travels

Unfortunately, in the forest, the direction of a sound can be very deceptive. It can sound right up close by when it really is far away. It can sound like it is coming from the left side, when really it is coming from right and center.

It was this way with the shotgun blasts.

Hank and Bronze headed off in what they both thought was the right direction, but was, in fact, the opposite.

Candy Krauss, with Doggo in tow, and Sunny Sanchez also heard the blasts and began to move in the opposite direction, only to find that they, too, were mistaken.

"What the hell—?" Sunny said as he backed into a dark form.

"Just keep quiet and no one gets hurt," said the man.

"Ouch!" Candy complained as the man grabbed her arm and pulled her roughly. Doggo barked.

"Shut up that mutt or I'll do it for you," the man snapped.

"Okay, quiet Doggo," Candy said and she put her hand around his muzzle.

"In front of me, where I can see you," said the man. "And remember, I've got the gun. In case you forget," Talenkov laughed.

"Who the hell—?" Sunny said again.

"None of your business. Keep walking and if you keep asking questions you'll get what he got."

Sunny and Candy stumbled onwards propelled by the prodding of the shotgun. They became accustomed to the dark so that the trees were more visible. The light between the trees made the sky like dark lace. They listened to their footsteps and were too panicked to wonder what was in store.

After walking for what seemed like half an hour Candy was thirsty. She kept bumping her feet against rocks and tree roots. She almost lost her footing several times and only Sunny holding on to her arm kept her upright.

"I suppose you think this makes you a big man," Sunny said.

"Shut up," said Talenkov and prodded him more forcefully with the gun.

The ground became more and more soggy. "It's a creek bed," Sunny said.

"I told you to shut up!" the man growled.

Then it happened

Candy stumbled over an exposed root. "Oww!" she yelled and Doggo jumped from her arms.

"Doggo!" she called out.

"Damn!" Talenkov screamed as Doggo bit his ankle. Sunny grabbed the shotgun. Talenkov grabbed for it back and in the struggle the gun went off. It was impossible to tell what was happening in the darkness. There was a cry and a body dropped to the ground.

"Sunny!" Candy cried.

"I'm okay," he said breathlessly. "I got him. Where's Doggo?"

They heard a yip and Sunny reached down and picked up the small hero. "Guess you know what's what, huh?" he said warmly. Doggo licked his face.

"Oh, Sunny, I'm so glad you're all right!" Candy cried. She tried to embrace both man and dog.

"Hey, watch it!" Sunny said as he leaned the shotgun against a tree.

"Where does this leave us?" Candy asked after they had all embraced. Twice.

Sunny touched the body with the butt of the gun. The man was definitely dead. Sunny found a flash in the pocket of his coat.

"Who is this?" he asked as he trained the light on the dead man's face.

"I guess since he was trying to kill us he's the enemy?" Candy suggested.

"I guess so," Sunny agreed.

Doggo was inspecting the ground. He barked.

"What did you find, O Brave One?" Sunny asked and flashed the light where Doggo was sniffing.

"Oh my god! Get out of here! Take Doggo! Now!" Sunny commanded.

"What is it?" asked Candy, snatching up the still curious dog.

"Just run!" Sunny grabbed her hand and dragged her along.

"But—" Candy gasped.

"Not now!" Sunny yelled.

They reached a clearing with a large rock.

"Behind here," he pulled Candy and Doggo alongside. "Cover your head," he said.

A flash of light filled the sky as the unexploded grenade went off.

"Oh my god!" Candy whispered. "Oh my god!"

"Doggo, you saved us again," Sunny said.

"What happened?" Candy asked.

"An unexploded hand grenade. Maybe left over from some war. Or maybe it was some terrorist. I remember reading that the Bahamian police found an unexploded grenade inside the office of one of their newspapers. Someone threw it in the door. This was a couple of years back."

"So what was the grenade doing here?" Candy asked.

"Beats me," said Sunny. "Sometimes if they're left alone for a period of time the mechanism in them starts to decay and the slightest thing can set them off. Best to call the cops. Lucky Doggo found it or we might be part of the fireworks."

Another escape

Hackerstein had just been plain lucky to escape Taleknov's shotgun. Well, not totally. Talenkov   had wounded Hackerstein's leg and he was limping, leaving a trail of blood. He went as fast as he could, in the direction he thought was away from the wreck. There seemed to be light in between the trees coming from one direction. Could it be a road? As he walked on and on the silence of the forest seemed overwhelming. The pounding of the blood in his ears was deafening and his breathing was difficult. He was gulping for air. The last thing he had in mind after having escaped not only the plane wreck and the clutches of the fake huntsman was the Russian, who would have left him to die alone in the forest.

"Keep on, Henry, keep on," he said to himself. "Remember Henriette, remember Henriette.

"Henriette, dear, without you there is no way this world has any meaning anymore. Whatever I did I did for you. I couldn't stand seeing you in all that pain any longer. I planned to take the money and get us to a better place.

"When I came to visit the other night in the assisted living you were sleeping in a big lounge chair in the common room. There was a lady who used to be a your table at lunch.

"'You should have heard your wife last night,' she said. 'She kept crying out for you. "Henry! Henry! If only I could hold you in my arms once more before I die!" She said it over and over.'

"Well, it broke my heart when she told me that. I tried to wake you, Henreitte, and I did eventually but you were asleep pretty deeply. I guess the medication does that. And I kissed you and held you. So I want you to know that whatever happens to me now, you got your wish.

"And I got my wish to be married to the best girl in the world. You will always be that for me. I don't want you to give it a second thought. I've been planning this and I didn't tell you because I didn't want you to have any part of it. I know you would have tried to stop me, but I couldn't go on alone without you. So if you have to go on without me for a little while, know that I am waiting for you with open arms and open heart."

Hackerstein tripped over a rock and the pain brought him back from his reverie.

"Why had Mr. Dylan sent that man to kill me?" Hackerstein asked himself as he made his way through the darkness. "And who was that other man? He said it was his job to kill me. Why?" He didn't want to remember his massive gambling debts that he had been keeping a secret from his wife. They had caused him to go to a loan shark and then, when he couldn't pay, the loan shark had some other idea.

The loan shark sat at this desk eating a sandwich.

"You work for the airlines, yes?" the loan shark asked. He was a short, fat, balding man who wore a toupee. Although Hackerstein didn't want to admit it, he knew the man was "connected" and that he was with the Russian mob. At first he put aside his fears of how dangerous it could be; he had heard all kinds of stories, even seen TV episodes about the Russian mob.

"How much worse can they be than the Mafia?" he had asked himself. "How much worse than having the bank foreclose on the house and losing everything?" He had pictured the humiliation, having to tell Henriette that all their retirement money, and more, was gone and never coming back.

He soon learned. The Russian mob didn't want just money, they wanted information about flights, payrolls coming in on the airlines. He thought it would be easy to give them what they wanted, and at first it was. Then he realized when he had paid up what he owed, they were still not letting him stop.

That's why when Mrs. Krutz had offered him a different kind of deal, hijacking the plane in return for substantial cash and a new identity, he fairly jumped at the chance. He hadn't told Henriette where the cash was coming from. "A big bonus for all the years of my loyal service," was how he put it. Now he saw what that loyal service had gotten him: a target painted on his back, a shot in the leg and this nightmare in the woods at night.

"At least it's better than being killed," he thought and he shuddered with the cold. The night air had begun to get to him. Before he was so filled with adrenaline that he didn't feel a thing; now the damp was having its effect.

He finally had to stop and bind up his leg; the pain was too intense. He remembered a tourniquet, but he didn't know how to do it. He took off his necktie and tied it around the thigh, above the wound.

"It's the best I can do," he said to himself.

Then he heard it: sound of the ambulance. At first he thought he was imagining it. But the sound was coming from where the light was and the light was increasing.

"A road? A highway?" he thought. And he went as rapidly as he could toward what he hoped was his salvation.

Two more woodland wanderers

Hank and Bronze heard the shot fired between Talenkov and Sunny Sanchez. They thought it was Hackerstein and someone else. But who? They moved rapidly in the direction of the sounds.

Then came the explosion. Luckily they were not closer.

"What was that?" Bronze asked. Hank shook his head.

They went around the burning underbrush toward the clearing which was open to the sky.

When they reached Candy and Sunny, they were totally bewildered.

"How did you two get here?" Bronze asked.

"Doggo ran away," Candy explained, "and Sunny helped me look for him."

"Then we found this guy that killed some other guy in the woods, or he found us." Sunny indicated direction of the dead Talenkov. Sunny said, "He was taking us somewhere when Doggo—"

"Doggo saved the day!" Candy interrupted. "He bit his ankle, the man dropped the gun and Sunny struggled with him."

"Well, something like that," Sunny said. "Then Doggo found an unexploded grenade."

"Ahha!" Bronze nodded in comprehension.

"Good work." Hank patted Sunny on the back.

"And what about Doggo?" Candy insisted.

"Good dog, good dog," Hank scratched Doggo behind the ears.

"He loves that," said Candy.

"So does my dog," Hank admitted.

"But where is Hackerstein?" Bronze asked.

"Who's Hackerstein?" Candy asked.

Bronze and Hank exchanged glances.

"The air marshal, he has a government cell phone," Bronze said cautiously.

"I didn't know there was an air marshal on the plane," Candy exclaimed.

"That's the whole point," Sunny said. "You're not supposed to recognize him. So if someone is a terrorist the air marshal can surprise him."

"Great job he did," Hank couldn't help but comment.

"So where is he now?" Candy asked.

"We were hoping that he was with you," Bronze said. "Did you see anyone else around here? Did you hear anything else?"

"We were kind of busy trying not to be shot," Sunny said. "We didn't really think there was anyone else around."

"Now you two kids, can you find your way back to the plane?" Bronze asked. "I can point you in the general direction."

"I guess," said Candy.

"Here," said Hank, pulling out what looked to be a pocket watch from his pants pocket. "It's a compass." He explained to Sunny how to use it and gave his estimation of where the plane should be.

"Eventually you'll hear the noise of the ambulances, and see the lights," Bronze said with a confidence he did not totally feel.

"Will you be okay?" Candy asked.

"We're the ones that should be asking you that," Hank said and laughed.

Onwards

Hank and Bronze waited until the sounds of Candy's and Sunny's footsteps disappeared.

"They didn't even ask who Talenkov was," Bronze remarked.

"Who was he?" Hank asked.

"Oh, I thought you knew. He was part of the Russian mob, a hired killer," Bronze said. "Let's go," and he started out.

"And you know this because—?" Hank asked as he followed.

"Well, he came up front and tried to help us," Bronze said. "And I finally recognized him from some of the circulars at the station. But I guess there are some things that will never be fully explained."

"I sure missed a lot by being with the regular passengers." Hank shook his head in amazement.

"Be thankful you did; no one needs this," Bronze said.

"This is what I signed on for, being a cop," Hank complained.

"I guess," Bronze said. He was not really interested in anything resembling small talk. "Shhh," he said to Hank.

Hank fell silent.

More ambulances

"I would really feel more comfortable in an ambulance," Olivia Livingston persisted.

"Mother, you are not injured. The ambulances are for the injured." Karen objected.

"Well, I'm old and at my age the injury may not be apparent at first," Olivia suggested.

"In that case, why don't you two ride along in the next ambulance?" Chief Lockwood said.

"A gentleman at last." Olivia gave the chief one of her most winning smiles.

"Dr. Lee," said Chief Lockwood, "why don't you see where you can fit Mrs. Livingston and her daughter in one of the next transports."

Dr. Wendy Lee was assigning the injured in order of the most serious.

"Sure thing," said Dr. Lee. "Why don't you two ladies rest here for the moment." She indicated a folding chair for Mrs. Livingston and an overturned crate for her daughter.

"Doctor!" came a call from Captain Stark. "Here!" He had just separated a body out of the pile of the dead that had been retrieved from the plane. "I think he's still breathing."

The body was charred almost beyond recognition. The clothes were burned and it was impossible to tell if the person were male or female.

"I think it's my wife." A tall man in a wet raincoat standing alongside was desperate. "Can you save her?"

"What do you think, Doctor?" Stark asked as Dr. Lee shone a small flashlight on the motionless form.

Dr. Lee shook her head no. "I'm sorry, Captain, but it's too late."

Stark took the man aside. "I'm sorry but I don't think we can do anything," said Stark. He guided him to sit on a crate. "We can't even be certain it's your wife."

The tall man put his head in his hands. "I just can't believe it would come to this," he sobbed.

Dr. Lee put a reassuring hand on his shoulder. "Captain, you and your crew have done all that is humanly possible to rescue those who had half a chance. You cannot blame yourself, nor can you reverse the order of events."

Stark just shook his head. "If only I had gotten the controls away from her earlier."

"You must not blame yourself, Captain. We do not have the luxury now of despair if we are to be of use to the living."

"Thank you, Doctor, I guess you're right." Stark stood up and began to survey those who remained at the scene.

"Captain, there's a woman here who needs immediate assistance." It was Happy Charles and he was helping Ethiopia Beldez who was limping. Her arm also seemed to be broken. She was crying out in pain.

"Into the next transport," Stark said and he guided Charles and Ethiopia towards Dr. Lee and the waiting ambulance.

"Easy does it," said Dr. Lee and she handed the woman up into the vehicle.

"And don't forget us!" Olivia Livingston called out.

"Of course not," Dr. Lee said as she helped the two women in also. "Safe journey," she said as she closed the doors of the transport.

More surprises

Dr. Lee had been so busy getting people sorted out, taken care of and ministering to those whose needs were not critical, that she hadn't had time to really take in her surroundings. Now with just a moment to breathe, she walked a few steps back from the center of the action and took a long look.

Strange she hadn't noticed that the ambulances did not bear the name of the nearby towns. They were the size of the usual ambulance, but they were covered in camouflage, like army trucks. And the medics didn't have the usual uniforms.

"The haste, the emergency of it," she reasoned to herself. She walked over to Sheriff Lockwood.

"I see that the ambulances look like they've come from the nearby army base," she said by way of making conversation.

"We were lucky," Sheriff Lockwood said, "that they could lend them to us. A small town like ours isn't really prepared for a disaster of this proportion."

"I guess not," said Dr. Lee.

"Doctor, please," came a call from Zedda Stein. She was choking.

"Give her some oxygen," Dr. Lee directed the medic. "Breathe slowly, now," she said as she took her pulse. "I think she'll be all right," she said to the sheriff.

"Maybe you should go along with her to the hospital, just to be sure," Sheriff Lockwood suggested. "We're almost through here, unfortunately," he indicated the mounting pile of the dead.

Dr. Lee took another look. It seemed as if there was a significantly larger number of additional bodies than there had been half an hour ago. "Efficient rescue efforts," she thought to herself, and yet she hadn't noticed any renewed activity around the wrecked plane.

As she was getting her small carry bag to board the ambulance, she noticed that another of the rescue vehicles had circled back around. Instead of coming front to take on more victims, it had parked by the pile of the dead. The doors opened and two people got out and began to unload bodies, adding them to the pile of the plane crash victims. The bodies were in light colored clothing, not dark like those that had been burned.

"Maybe I should stay on for the last survivors," Dr. Lee said to the sheriff.

"As you wish," Sheriff Lockwood said.

The ambulance Dr. Lee had noticed then pulled up to take on more passengers. Dr. Lee saw yet another ambulance pulling up to the pile of corpses and unloading bodies. Then it got in line to take on more passengers.

"Here we go," Sheriff Lockwood handed Holly Nash and James Cologne into the ambulance.

"But I really feel okay now," Holly protested.

"Can't be too careful," the sheriff said. "And you go with her, young man," he indicated James Cologne.

"My plan, too," James said as he helped hand Holly into the transport.

"You, too, Dr. Lee," said the sheriff. "I think we can handle it from here."

Dr. Lee took one last look at the scene of the disaster and climbed in behind Holly and James. Sheriff Lockwood shut the doors and pulled the handle down tight.

Tracking time

Bronze and Hank closed in on what they assumed was Hackerstein. They were so close they could hear his footsteps crunching the underbrush.

"Yuck," Hank said softly. He had just been smeared with some liquid and when he put his hand closer to his face, he saw that it was blood. "He's wounded," he whispered to Bronze.

They were silent. Soon they could detect the uneven tread of a man limping.

Hank pulled his gun and nodded to Bronze. "You get ready to go around the other side of him, in case he runs," he said. "He won't go far."

Hank speeded up slightly and as soon as Hackestein was in his sights he yelled, "Freeze! Police!"

Hackerstein began to hobble as fast as he could straight ahead to what he saw as a service road. A car went by and the headlights illuminated the road briefly before disappearing around another curve.

Hank was gaining on him and fired a warning shot. "Freeze, you bastard!" he yelled.

Hackerstein just kept on running. If only he could make it to the roadway. His leg was almost numb, like a tree limb that he was dragging. Then he saw the headlights of another car. Luck was with him.

He hobbled out of the edge forest, onto the pavement. He wouldn't look back. He couldn't afford to lose the time. If that copper was going to shoot him, then he was going to be shot. Nothing he could do about that. If he were too slow, the car wouldn't see him . Luck again! It was an ambulance probably from the crash site. He stepped firmly into the road so that the van couldn't help but see him and would have to stop or run him over.

The last transport

"Well, we're lucky!" said Cologne. "You're the doctor that saved that guy with the heart attack, aren't you?"

"Yes, that's me," said Dr. Lee. She was watching the medic give Holly an oxygen mask.

"I'm all right, really," she protested.

"Just to be on the safe side," the medic said and fastened the elastic around the back of her head. "Take deep breaths. You, too," he said and gave Cologne a mask.

"Couldn't hurt, I guess," James accepted the oxygen mask.

Dr. Lee put out a hand to stop him. "Unnecessary medication can increase your resistance to medication when you might need it in the future."

"Not the case here, Doctor," said the medic and pushed Dr. Lee's hand away. The medic began to put the mask on James Cologne again.

As Dr. Lee pushed the hand of the medic away from James she saw that Holly Ash was starting to choke. She clutched her throat. Dr. Lee tore the mask off of her.

"James!" she yelled. "It's not oxygen!"

Cologne struggled with the medic as Dr. Lee pulled Holly free of the noxious fumes. She found the valve on the tank and turned the poison off.

Cologne punched the medic but the medic was not as fragile as he looked. He pulled out a hypodermic and lunged at Cologne.

"Duck!" Dr. Lee yelled as she pushed Holly out of the way.

James was looking to punch the medic without getting stuck by the needle. Dr. Lee maneuvered to nab the medic by a pressure point in his neck, causing him to drop the hypodermic. James grabbed the man's arms behind him while Dr. Lee took some surgical tubing and quickly tied his hands.

"What's going on back there?" the driver of the vehicle yelled. He began to turn around to look and at that point there was a thud and everyone lurched forwards.

The last victim?

Hackerstein felt the impact of the ambulance briefly as his body went under.

"Let us out!" Dr. Lee yelled but the driver didn't stop. Dr. Lee climbed from the back into the front seat and grabbed the steering wheel. The two struggled.

"James!" Dr. Lee called out.

Cologne got in back of the driver and began to choke him until he went limp. Dr. Lee yanked the wheel and stepped on the brake. With James' help, Dr. Lee pushed the driver out of the seat, put the van in park and got out.

"He wanted to kill that man!" Holly cried. "He didn't stop! He wanted to kill him!"

Dr. Lee got out of the van.

"I'm afraid to say this man is dead," she said after examining Hackerstein's bloody body.

"What is going on?" Cologne asked, emerging from the van.

"I hate to say this, but I think that these are not rescue vehicles," Dr. Lee said as she tied the hands of the unconscious driver with surgical tubing. "Give me some help here," she said to James and they dragged both fake medics to the side of the road.

"I noticed that the ambulances were returning to the crash site and adding bodies to the pile of corpses," Dr. Lee explained. "They were killing those that were supposed to go to the hospitals. And they were bringing the bodies back to the pile of accident victims."

"Just like they tried to kill me!" Holly exclaimed.

"Exactly," said Dr. Lee.

"And me," said James with disbelief. "But why?"

"Possibly someone in a high position of power does not want anyone that was on the flight to remain alive," Dr. Lee said.

"You got that right," said Bronze as he and Hank stepped from the forest out onto the road.

"I'm the co-pilot, Billy Bronze," Bronze introduced himself. "This is Hank, one of the law enforcement officers on the plane." They shook hands.

"I don't think we have a lot of time here," Bronze continued. "Let's get these bodies into the forest and get going."

The last ride

Once inside the van, Bronze began to explain. "What you saw, Doctor, that puts it all in a different light. The government was trying to cover up what happened on the plane."

"And what happened exactly? Someone please fill me in," Cologne interrupted.

"There was a terrorist who planted a bomb," Bronze said.

"How could they get it past airport security?" Holly asked.

"By working along with the air marshal," Bronze explained. "And probably working with someone in the ground crew. The person on the ground could have added some hardware to the plane's computer system and some software too. They also could have planted the bag with the bomb inside the plane. Then the air marshal monkeyed with the avionics and rigged up the computer to control the plane. But the terrorist on the flight ended up double crossing the air marshal and those who hired her; the bomb went into the ocean. It might have hit a stray tanker that got caught in the storm."

"But who hired her?" asked Holly.

"Someone in the government," Bronze continued. "Probably some extreme right winger. They wanted to provoke Cuba into bombing an American plane, but they didn't want the terrorist identified as hired by the American government. That way the Cubans would be the bad guys."

"That was why there were no jets accompanying us when we found out there was a bomb on board!" Cologne exclaimed.

"Exactly," Bronze said. "When the control tower found out that we had an emergency, a terrorist on board, they would have sent out planes to escort us. If there had been planes alongside it would have been an acknowledgement by our government that we weren't responsible for the actions of the plane. The government would have had to work with the Cuban government, making the Cubans look like good guys."

"But the bomb didn't go off over Cuba. I still don't understand," Holly said.

"Right. So the mission failed. The only way to avoid the truth coming out was to destroy those involved. In this case, everyone on the plane," Bronze concluded.

"So she was a cyber terrorist! I knew something funny was happening with the computer system when the lights in the plane went off. It was all connected!" Cologne said.

"Exactly," Bronze continued.

The van was speeding along. Dr. Lee was driving.

"Long story short. Since she couldn't fly the plane, we crashed. The air marshal escaped. That is, until just now when this van hit him accidentally on purpose. The government is afraid that if those of us who survived the crash tell our stories, people will put things together and find out the truth."

"Which is?" Cologne persisted.

"The truth is that the government must have been the one to hire the terrorist to begin with," said Bronze. "They want to throw suspicion on Cuba."

"I can't believe this!" Holly exclaimed.

"Neither can I," said Hank. "It's too incredible."

"How could they do this to us? I mean it's our government," Holly continued.

"You just saw how they could do this. It's not a pretty picture," said Bronze.

No one said anything.

"Well, do you have another explanation to fit all the facts?" Bronze asked. "I think that what Dr. Lee saw, the bodies being unloaded from the ambulances and added to the crash site victims, sort of clinches it. Either they died en route or they were taken somewhere and killed."

There was a silence.

Then something ran out in front of the van. Dr. Lee slammed on the brakes. Everyone jolted forward.

Two people ran out of the forest.

"Doggo!" It was Candy Krauss and Sunny Sanchez. "Doggo!" she yelled and picked up the small animal. "You could have hit him!" she yelled.

"But I didn't," said Dr. Lee. "I recognize you from the plane."

"We got lost in the woods," Sunny explained. "And we discovered your dead convict," he said to Hank.

"What happened to you guys?" Candy asked.

"It's a long story," Hank said.

"Where do we go from here?" Dr. Lee asked. "What if the local law enforcement stops us?"

"The nearest airport is our best bet," suggested Bronze. "If my calculations are correct we've landed in the Bahamas where we were headed all along."

"We sure took the long way around," Candy said.

Doggo barked in agreement.

The news report

DC flight 787 from JFK to Nassau in the Bahamas crashed last night at approximately 6:45 PM. All 237 passengers on board and the crew were reported killed. The causes of the crash are held to be engine failure due to inclement weather pending further investigation. Among the passengers was the well-known romance novelist, Enid Snark, noted for her series, "The Wings of My Heart" and celebrity Helmut Hardcastle, a popular shopping channel host.

Made in United States
Orlando, FL
30 March 2022

16317770R00150